WALKER BRIDE
BOOK 3
THE WALKER FAMILY SERIES

BY
BERNADETTE MARIE

This is a fictional work. The names, characters, incidents, places, and locations are solely the concepts and products of the author's imagination or are used to create a fictitious story and should not be construed as real.

5 PRINCE PUBLISHING AND BOOKS, LLC
PO Box 16507
Denver, CO 80216
www.5PrinceBooks.com

ISBN-10: 1-63112-154-5ISBN 13: 978-1-63112-154-8
WALKER BRIDE
Bernadette Marie
Copyright Bernadette Marie, 2015
Published by 5 Prince Publishing

Front Cover designed by Bernadette Soehner
Author Photo: Brenden Murphy, 2015

First Edition/First Printing February 2016 Printed U.S.A.

5 PRINCE PUBLISHING AND BOOKS, LLC.

Stan,
Everything started the day I became your bride.

Acknowledgements:

To my boys: There are no words for how proud I am of you. Future spouses will be well taken care of because you are amazing men.

To my husband: Only lucky wives have the support of their husbands in whatever they choose to do. I'm the luckiest.

To my mom, dad, and sister: I'm grateful for my internal village which makes me seem like the well put together wife and mother. I love you.

To Connie, Clare, and June: Between short deadlines, crazy ideas, and missed emails, we sure do take amazing journeys together. Thank you for humoring me through them.

To my wonderful readers: You are all the most amazing people. I love getting to know those of you who reach out to me. You make my job the very best.

Dear Reader,

I can't help but being a sucker for a family saga. I love when families are mixed together and dynamics differ.

I think that is exactly what I have built with the Walkers. Each side is immensely different than the other.

Of course, it's always good to throw in a generations-long battle between another prominent family—enter the Morgans.

You might imagine I had some fun stirring the pot and mixing Pearl Walker and Tyson Morgan together. As an author, I tend to write the kinds of stories I enjoy reading.

With that said, I hope you enjoy this installment of the Walker Family Series with Walker Bride.

Happy Reading!
Bernadette Marie

Other books by Bernadette Marie

WALKER BRIDE

Chapter One

Ivory satin was smooth under her fingers. Each pin held the hem of the bride's dream dress in its mermaid style.

Pearl Walker carefully let go of the fabric and made clear notes for the seamstress. There could be no miscommunications when it came to this dress. This dress had to be perfect because it would belong to Pearl's sister Bethany.

The dress that hung in its bag just beyond her, on the rack, was for her cousin's future bride, Susan. That made two Walker brides having weddings in a span of two months. Who was next, she wondered.

Her vote was on Lydia Morgan, her cousin Eric's other cousin, and a childhood friend of hers. Well, perhaps Pearl shouldn't consider they were friends back then. Lydia was studious, and Pearl was a little bit of a wild child. Though, she thought, as she looked in the full-length mirror to her right, she certainly didn't look like one now.

Her suit was Vera Wang, and it made her look the part of a successful business woman, who owned a bridal boutique. She kept her hair pinned up. That too, made her look smart, she thought. Pearls had replaced the black rubber bracelets that had lined her arm long ago. A French manicure gave her nails a clean look, not like the black paint of years ago. A tattoo on her thigh hid beneath her skirt, but there were traces of the bad girl that was still lingering under the blonde façade of the business woman.

She heard the bell over the front door of her shop chime. Careful not to drop Bethany's dress, she stood and walked to the front.

Standing, all six-foot-four of him, very uncomfortable with his hands in the front pockets of his jeans, was Eric's half-brother Tyson Morgan.

"Hey, Ty. Did you come to get fitted for that tux finally?"

"Yeah. Don't know why they want me in their wedding. Don't they have professionals to do that?"

She smiled sweetly as she studied him. He was a country boy, that was for sure. He wore worn out work boots and faded jeans. His T-shirt might have seen better days and his hair peeked out around the edges of his baseball cap, which also got plenty of wear.

"They chose you to be in the wedding because you're important to them," she said.

"I spent most my life hating the Walker family, no offense."

"None taken."

"Who could have known I was related to one? Damn if that makes the least bit of sense ever, huh?"

"Come on back. Let's get you measured."

She walked toward her fitting area with the three-way mirror and platform. As she gathered her tape measure, she thought about that Walker-Morgan feud. It had been fueled for as long as she could remember, started over land rights early at the turn of last century, and the battle had continued until about ten months ago. It had been quite a shock to Tyson to find that the mother that abandoned him had been the same woman who married into the Walker family— Eric's mother. She'd been a troubled soul, but forty years later her mistakes had brought the two families together.

Now here stood the handsome Morgan man in her bridal shop. Truly this was something Pearl had never thought would happen either.

"What size are your shoes?"

A flash of annoyance crossed over Tyson's face. "Why?"

Pearl affixed her professional smile. "I carry a stock of dress shoes in back. If I take your measurements in the appropriate shoes, then I can assure that the tuxes will fit correctly."

"What's wrong with my boots?"

Keeping the smile in place, she replied, "Susan has requested that all the groomsmen wear dress shoes."

"Well, hell, no one mentioned that."

"Honestly, it won't take but a moment here. What size?"

She was sure he blurted out the number thirteen. She gave him a nod and disappeared into the back of the store to find the appropriately sized shoe.

Men were usually more uncomfortable taking off their shoes in front of her than they were to take off their clothes. She could only assume that Tyson would be the same.

He was turned away from the mirror when she returned. She handed him the box containing the shoes.

"Here you go. Try these."

"I really think it would be fine if we…"

"Can I get you a soda or a bottle of water?" Men were also usually more comfortable with a bottle in their hands. Though she steered from keeping beer in the store, this was something she had studied.

"Uh, sure. Coke?"

"You put on the shoes. I'll get you one."

Again, she left him alone in the dressing area and ducked into the back room to retrieve the drink. Her refrigerator was full of sodas and water. She specifically purchased soda in bottles so that men could have that feel in their hands. If it were a woman she was trying to ease, she'd have poured the soda into a fancy glass with ice.

When she figured she'd given him enough time, she walked back into the dressing area.

"Here you go," she handed over the bottle and smiled, acknowledging the shoes that were now on his feet.

"Thanks." He took the soda and twisted off the top. "Do you have men in here a lot?" he asked as he squirmed under her assessing look.

"Everyday. It's a natural event here. But like I said, you'll be out in a few moments."

She draped the tape measure around the back of her neck and retrieved her measurement notebook and a pencil.

"I'm going to start with your shoulders."

He gave her a grunt of approval, and she went to work.

Seriously, no one had ever asked him to do anything so uncomfortable in his entire life. And here he was, standing in a dress shop, in borrowed shoes, letting a Walker measure him.

In the mirror, he watched her move a step stool into place behind him and step up. She took the tape measure from around her neck, then ran it from one side of his shoulders to the other. The tingle of her fingers resonated through his shirt and down through his skin.

He bit down hard to control his body from flinching, gripping tightly to the bottle of soda in his hand.

"Now, I'll do your arm," her voice was soft, and her breath was warm on his neck.

She held her hand at the top of his shoulder and just as she'd done across his back, she slid her hand delicately down his arm until she reached his wrist.

How quickly did she say this was going to take? Tyson was thinking he'd need a much stiffer drink than soda when she was done measuring him.

Moving to the other arm, and then his chest, it gave him the chance to catch the scent of her perfume.

Tyson clenched his toes in the borrowed shoes and closed his eyes as she reached her arms around his waist, her body brushing against his.

She took the measurement quickly and then wrote it down in the notebook she'd laid at her feet.

"Why couldn't I just tell you my pant size and my coat size? You have to measure everyone?" he asked, noticing she was kneeling before him and not rising.

Every person is built differently, even if they are the same size," she said, using air quotes to emphasize her point.

Well, now how was he supposed to take that comment with her reaching her hands toward his crotch?

Realizing he was thinking just a bit too much about where her hands were going to travel, he stumbled back, nearly falling from the small platform she had him standing on.

"Sorry. I guess this is making me a little uncomfortable."

She smiled sweetly up at him. He didn't think it was possible to like a Walker, let alone find one extremely attractive, but damn if those blue eyes weren't burning right through him.

"Two more measurements," she promised.

Tyson clenched his fists at his side and closed his eyes as he felt her hand on the inside of his thigh.

"Okay, all done."

He realized he held his breath too.

"Good."

She stood and made her notes. "You can change your shoes back now."

He gave her a nod and went to the nearest chair to sit, setting the bottle of soda on the small table between the chairs. "You do that every day? I mean, isn't that like feeling up men for a living?"

She chuckled. "If that's what you think I was doing."

Yeah, that was exactly what he was thinking of her doing—what she was doing, that was.

He pulled off the shoes and tucked them into the box.

"I kinda think I need a drink now." He'd said it louder than he'd meant to and he noticed her smiling and the heat in her cheeks. Maybe he should have kept it to himself.

"I'll let Susan know all the tuxes have been measured for," she said turning toward him.

"I was the last one, huh?"

"You were my hold out. I thought I was going to have to come out to your house. This might be cause for some celebration."

Now he could feel the heat rise in his cheeks. Having his body measured at her store was bad enough. Had she done that in his house...well, it was better just to stop thinking about it because now, looking at her in her perfect suit, the image what they could have done was too vivid.

"Well, I guess we're done. I should go," he said after he pulled on his boots.

She looked up at him, those blue eyes burning right into him. The shimmering gloss on her lips only accentuated the fullness of them.

God, what was he thinking?

"Are you still going for that drink?" she asked, and he had to think about what he'd said to prompt that.

"Oh, right. The drink. I think I'd better." Her eyes were still locked on him. "Would you like to join me?"

He watched as she licked her lips, then bit down on the bottom one with her perfectly white teeth. "I thought you'd never ask. Let me get my things."

His lungs began to burn, and he realized again, he was holding his breath as he watched her walk away. What was he doing? Pearl Walker had a certain reputation he remembered. And he'd just been felt up by the prim and proper version.

This just might end up being the most interesting night of his life.

Chapter Two

It had been worth inviting herself to tag along just to see Tyson's expression, Pearl thought. Okay, she might have made his experience getting fitted for a tux a little too intimate. He didn't know it wasn't *the norm* and in no way did she violate him at all. She was just having some fun.

Tyson Morgan had always been a mystery to her. Of course, he was the older brother of her friend Lydia, and he was off limits to any Walker to get to know for years. That feud between her father, grandfather, and uncle with his grandfather had simply been ego—or pride. Pearl couldn't have been more surprised when it came out that Tyson was actually her cousin Eric's half-brother. That only made him more intriguing. Mystery shrouded him, and Pearl liked a mystery.

She also liked tall, muscular men who wore boots and ball caps. It didn't hurt anything that he was twelve years older too. She liked them a little more seasoned than herself though she was no prude.

Pearl gave herself one last look in the mirror that hung over the sink in the back room. Fetching her lipstick out of her purse, she slid it over her lips, then pressed them together. She looked like a million bucks, she thought. Oh, she'd come a long way from the heavy eyeliner, ear piercings, and black hair. She had her mother's blonde hair. Desecrating it with jet black color made her skin look so pale, she nearly appeared dead. That had pissed her parents off. Of course, that had been the point.

Heavy metal had blared from her stereo, and there was always a stash of stolen alcohol in the bottom of her closet. Not to mention she'd spent all of her money on fancy clove cigarettes.

That made her laugh. Now she drank champagne and nibbled on chocolate-covered strawberries with clients. The salon had a standing appointment for her hair and nails. Over the years, she'd become a fashionable and significant member of society.

Still, there was a little deviousness inside of her, and it had come out when that sexy Tyson Morgan walked in her door, and she'd draped the measuring tape across his broad shoulders. Work had taken over her life, especially lately since so many members of her family were getting married. It was time to let her hair down and have some fun. And it seemed as though her body was itching to have fun with Tyson. All she had to do was make her move and make him hers.

Tyson juggled his keys between his palms as he waited for Pearl to return from the back room. He needed to tell her he had too much to do. This wasn't going to happen—this drink he'd mentioned.

When she walked back into the room, he found that the man in him didn't have the courage to tell her goodbye. She was stunning. She didn't look any different than she had ten minutes earlier, except for fresh lipstick, but damn!

"Where should we go?" she asked, turning off the lights in the room.

He looked around. Even though it was still sunny outside, the room had nearly gone black.

"Um, I don't know. I didn't plan on this at all."

The smile that formed on her lips twisted his insides. "There's a little bar down the street. Local brewery."

"Alright."

"We can buy a sandwich from the deli next door and take it in."

"They let you do that?"

"That's how it works. It's a tap room, not a restaurant. You order food from the nearby restaurants. Sometimes they have a food truck." She cocked her hip, with her hand on it, and gave him a sultry gaze to go with the attitude. "You don't come to town too often do you?"

"Not if I can help it."

She smiled, and the white from her teeth nearly glowed in the dark room. Placing a manicured finger on his chest she moved in close. "Drinks and a late, late lunch is on me then. It's a special occasion."

"Why's that?"

"You're in town—finally getting fitted. It's Friday. And I don't have any more appointments today. Let's celebrate."

He let out a long steady breath as he followed her to the front of the store.

As soon as they walked through the front door, Pearl turned and locked the store up tight. He watched as she looked up at the sign and smiled. There was a lot of pride in her little store. He knew the look of pride.

"Ready?" She turned that smile toward him, and he nodded. The deli was only a block away. She strolled right in with a wave to the man behind the counter.

"Pearl!" he said as if they were dear friends.

"How are you today, George?"

"It's a fine day isn't it?"

She gave him a glance over her shoulder and turned back to the counter. "It sure is."

Just with the look and the sultry sound of her voice, Tyson felt the heat rise on the back of his neck. His brother made him get fitted for a tux, and now he was on display? This was crap, and he was going to let Eric know about it. He didn't need Eric's cousin hitting on him. He didn't need any woman hitting on him. How the hell had he gotten himself into this situation?

Pearl ordered one sandwich and asked them to cut it in half. Obviously, they were sharing the club, which was his favorite, but what if he'd wanted a whole sandwich?

She paid George, as she'd called him, and lingered her hand on his as she took her change. "See ya next week," she said with a small wave.

He followed her out of the deli.

"Eat here a lot?"

She shrugged. "Maybe once a week. I try to stop in for an iced tea every few days. It's good to keep in the good graces with the businesses around you. I even stop into the barber shop across the street and catch a basketball game if I'm hanging out at the shop on the weekend."

"Why?"

"It's neighborly," she said with a laugh in her voice. "Don't you do that?"

"I manage the ranch. My neighbors are ten miles away. And until this year, I'd never met them, let alone talk to them."

"I've always thought that was strange and interesting," she said as she walked into the brewery with a wave to the woman behind the bar.

The woman in a tight black T-shirt with the front cut to form a V in the crevice of her pushed up breasts reached over the bar to hug Pearl.

"Didn't expect you till later," she said.

Pearl gave her an easy laugh. "I got an offer to leave early. Elise, this is Tyson Morgan."

The woman extended her hand to him, and he took it only to find she had a serious grip.

"Morgan? The ranch about ten miles out of town?"

"Yeah," he said pulling his hand back and tucking it into his pocket.

"You're Lydia's brother?"

"That's me."

She grinned. "Love her. Who couldn't love a spitfire like that?"

He shouldn't be surprised that Lydia had made friends around town. Unlike him, she was never out at the ranch. If she could get away, she did.

Since the Morgans and the Walkers had reconciled their family feud, or, at least, it was simmered down, she spent a lot of her time at his brother Eric's riding a horse Tyson had bought her for her birthday, which she refused to keep on their family property. She thought it was *neighborly*. Now that he'd heard the word come from Pearl's lips, he wondered where Lydia might have gotten the idea.

He and Lydia were as different as they came. Of course at forty-two years old, finding out he had different parents than she did, that should explain it. Lydia was outgoing, and as the woman with the perky chest in the tight T-shirt said, she was a spitfire.

"What can I get you?" the woman asked.

"I'll have my usual," Pearl said, and the woman nodded.

"I'm at a loss here. Craft beers?"

Pearl smiled. "From very mild to stout."

"And you are?"

She licked her lips, and he clenched his teeth to keep from letting the subtle motion trigger his masculinity into a jolt.

"I'm mild."

He looked at the woman behind the bar who was waiting for an answer. "Give me what she's having."

The woman winked and turned to get their beers.

"Mild? You? Not what I would have pegged," Pearl said as she pulled her wallet from her purse.

"Might not be by the time I'm done," he smirked as he pulled his wallet out of his pocket. "I got this. You got the sandwich."

"I said it was my treat."

"Right. I'm feeling just a bit wrong about that, so I'll get the beer."

Pearl slid her wallet back into her purse. "Thank you, Mr. Morgan. I'm going to procure that table by the window. You bring the drinks."

He watched her walk away, and that too had been a treat he hadn't expected to enjoy. She had a sway in those hips that offered a little too much. However, if he hadn't had noticed, he wouldn't have felt manly. At this very moment, he needed to feel that way.

After the woman in the T-shirt set down the beers, he slid her the bills from his wallet. She thanked him, he picked up the beers and headed toward Pearl.

Pearl already had napkins laid out and the sandwich separated into two servings. Tyson set the beers down and then took his seat at the raised stool.

"Wouldn't you be more comfortable at a shorter table?" he asked.

"I kinda like sitting up here and looking down at everyone," she said grinning as she picked up her beer and took a long sip. "Oh, this is good."

She held her glass up toward him as if she were going to make a toast. She held it there until he picked up his and mimicked her move.

"To a Friday afternoon full of promise," she said.

"What kind of promise?"

She licked her lips again. "I don't know. Let's drink and find out."

Pearl tapped her glass to his and then drank. She'd taken at least two or three sips before he realized he still had his glass in the air and was watching her.

Oh, hell, he might as well enjoy this very awkward afternoon. God knew he wasn't coming to town again for a very long time. And it had been a long time since a woman seemed to throw herself in his path. What wasn't to enjoy about that? Except that this wasn't just some woman. This was Pearl Walker, daughter of Byron Walker. The man had little morals and caused everyone in his wake more problems than necessary.

But watching her pick up her sandwich and take a bite, nearly did him in. Tyson sipped his beer as he watched her and he was reasonably sure he knew exactly what kind of promise she was offering. What man couldn't see that?

The real choice would be whether he wanted to get involved in such a thing. This was his half-brother's cousin. Wasn't that a little too close to the family? He thought again. Really—no—they weren't related at all, but he was, at least, ten years older than she was. He didn't need that headache he thought, as he took another sip.

Pearl watched the people walking up and down the street as she took a sip from her beer. Of course, she might be watching the people, but her attention was on the long stare Tyson was giving her.

It hadn't been until she'd touched him that she realized she'd been working too hard. It had been a very long time since she'd let her hair down, so to speak, and just enjoyed an evening—or a man.

He was very visibly uncomfortable too. Still, she was enjoying that as well.

"What do you think of the beer?" she asked.

"Nice. Certainly could go for something a little stouter."

"They have it. There's a chocolate one, but I never make it through a whole glass."

"You come here a lot too? A neighborly thing?"

"You could say that. Bridal parties like to stick together. I get invited for drinks every so often. Brides tend to get attached to their bridal professionals. At least until the wedding," she said, and the hint of sadness was a bit too obvious for her, so she planted a smile on her lips. "I direct them here."

"Very *neighborly* of you."

"How come you don't come to town?"

"Why? A half hour to get here. I usually can send Lydia for whatever I would need."

"You two are very different."

"Understatement," he said as he finished his beer. "I didn't realize you two were so close."

Pearl shrugged. "We're not. She's involved in two different wedding parties. Goes back to what I said about people getting involved with the bridal professional."

He shook his head. "I don't think that's the case here. You, Susan, Bethany, and Lydia have a lot in common when it comes to event planning. You with wardrobe. Susan caters. Lydia is buying up the whole town where you can have a wedding. And I heard Bethany is a floral artist in the making when she's not trying to try her hand at writing books."

Pearl sat back in her seat, crossing her legs. "You pay a lot of attention for a man who doesn't like to be around people."

"I didn't say I didn't like people."

In his own way he had, she thought. "What are you guys planning for Eric's bachelor party?"

His eyes grew wide. "We have to do that?"

On a laugh, she leaned forward. "Yes. You have to do that. You'd better get Russell, Gerald, Ben, and Dane planning."

"Dane won't be any help. He moved away, remember?"

Pearl nodded. Of course, she remembered. She'd been at the going away party his mother had thrown for him. Tyson had been the missing guest.

How could she blame him? He might be Eric's brother, but he was still a Morgan, and the rest of them were Walkers.

A little tingle of excitement resonated in her chest when she thought about it that way. What would they all think if another Morgan and another Walker got involved?

Pearl watched him as he bit into his sandwich. Lust began to pump through her veins now. She always was one to go against the grain.

"You need another beer," she offered as she hopped off her chair.

"I think one is good enough."

"Let me buy you one."

He looked at his empty glass. "One more. But get me something a little manlier."

She gave him a wink and sauntered up to the bar, hoping his eyes were right where she'd wanted them.

Chapter Three

It was still early on a Friday afternoon, but the tap room was growing more crowded, Pearl noticed as she walked toward the bar to order them another set of drinks.

Elise leaned in over the bar toward her. "He is super sexy if you ask me," she said in a hushed tone.

"I think so too."

"You making a move on him? I thought Walkers and Morgans didn't speak."

Pearl shrugged. "Childish don't you think? And damn, he's no child."

Elise shook her head. "He ain't that. Another round?"

"Same for me. Something manlier for him."

Elise laughed. "I got that covered." She turned and filled two more glasses. "He should like this."

"Thanks," Pearl said as she laid the cash on the bar and picked up the glasses.

"Is he the one who ends up being the brother of your cousin?"

Pearl hadn't thought the city was so small, but gossip sure could spread. "Yeah, that's him."

"No wonder he looks so pained. That's some drama there," she said as another man approached the bar.

Drama would be her middle name, Pearl thought as she walked back to the table with the drinks. She'd been born under a cloud of it. They often talked about drama queens, but her father was the king of the drama.

She set the drinks on the table and climbed on her stool. Picking up her drink, she took a long sip.

"You look a little preoccupied," Tyson said as he pulled his glass toward him. "Something happen?"

Elise had surely put a damper on Pearl's mood though there was no reason for it. And Pearl wasn't the kind of woman to get worked up over it either, so why was she?

"Elise seems to think there's a lot of drama where you're concerned."

He choked on his sip of beer. "She what?"

"This city is smaller than I thought it was. She knows your Eric's brother."

"Well, that made it's way around pretty fast. No wonder I keep away from here, huh?"

"What the hell would it matter who your brother is anyway?" she continued. "So your family had secrets. What family doesn't?"

There was a thin smile that crept over his lips, and she was quick to catch it.

"What?"

He sat back in his chair. "You and I have to come from some of the most dramatic families around. I didn't know my past was so shrouded in drama, but your dad is quite famous for his."

And wasn't that what she'd just been thinking?

"What do you know about my father?" she quickly quipped.

Tyson leaned in with his arms on the table and his glass between the palms of his hands. "I know that his two ex-wives were best friends before and after he was married to them. I know that you and your sister Audrey, and your brothers, are very close in age. And I know he was infatuated with Bethany's mother before he knew what a basket case she was."

"I think we can forgive him for that one, don't you? I mean a beautiful actress is going to get a man's libido running."

"Only she had many men's libidos running. Even men my age."

Pearl winced. "Were you friends with Douglas Brant too?"

He shrugged. "I knew him. I knew he was seeing an older woman too. I just wouldn't have pegged it to be Bethany's mother. Nor would I have thought he was crazy enough to try and murder people."

That alone called for another long sip of her beer.

Douglas Brant had been just that man. He too had been as obsessed with her sister Bethany's mother, Violet Waterbury. When Bethany showed up, after their grandfather's death, and was the spitting image of her mother, that had sparked some deep seeded lust in the heart of Douglas Brant. He'd gone crazy enough over it that he'd begun killing off Eric and Tyson's cattle and messing with their property in hopes of getting closer to Bethany. In the end, he'd kidnapped her and burned Eric's house to the ground, with him inside. Luckily he'd made it out alive, and Bethany had shot Douglas Brant before he could do anything to her.

Tyson picked up his beer and lingered it near his lips. "Tell me about your dad and his wives. There's a story there."

"Of course, there is. My father is his own soap opera."

He chuckled. "Remember my mom had me, ditched me, my uncle raised me as his, and she ran off and had another baby with your uncle. I can say that we are two people that come from soap opera families. I can handle it."

She shook her head and laughed. "Maybe we're meant to be."

His eyes opened wide as he took a long sip from his glass. Okay, perhaps she'd scared him to death with that comment. She'd move on to the story of her father's wives.

"Let's see. The story began when my father was engaged to my brothers' mother, Naomi."

"But your brothers are younger than you."

"Drama. Remember, I'm shrouded in drama."

He laughed again. "Continue."

"He and my mother, Naomi's best friend, had an affair, and oops, here I am."

"She got pregnant while your father was engaged to her best friend?"

"Nice huh? Anyway, he married my mom. My sister was born a short fifteen months later. He left all of us, married Naomi and quickly had Jake and Todd."

"A man on a mission, huh?"

"I guess. They divorced a couple of years later and then Bethany's mom came along. But he never married her."

"But your mom and Naomi are still good friends."

"They are now. I guess they bonded over how horrible a man Byron Walker is."

He leaned in again. "You think your father is a horrible man?"

"He's no upstanding citizen. Look what he did with my grandfather's land. He gambled it away."

"Yes, but that ended up being a scam."

"But your family almost had everything my family had worked for."

And there was the stickler to the whole Morgan/Walker feud.

He watched her carefully now and she couldn't decide if he was intrigued or disgusted.

She picked up her beer and drank it down. "Well, I guess I had more of an issue with it than I thought," she said. "I'm going to get another one. You want one?"

He looked down at his half empty glass and shook his head. "I'll be fine. I have a longer drive home."

"Right. Well, I'm thinking I need another."

She hopped off the stool and went to order another drink. At that moment, she wished they served something stronger than beer, though craft beer was plenty strong in her opinion.

Another waitress took her order, and she waited.

Her intentions on bringing Tyson to the bar had been to ease him into something—anything. She'd had her blood pumping since he'd walked through her door. What she hadn't anticipated was diving into family history and it upsetting her as much as it did.

She was no prude. She understood relationships and sex. Greed fueled her too. That's why she was so successful. What she didn't understand was a man who would move from woman to woman and family to family as if it were okay. Why would he think it was okay to gamble away their savings over and over and then try and take away what his father and his brother worked so hard to grow?

The waitress set her beer on the counter, and she picked it up with shaking hands.

The afternoon was going to be a waste now. Tyson Morgan was going to finish his drink and get out of there as fast as he could. Why wouldn't he? Crazy Walker women were not a prize to be won.

She could feel the first two beers swimming in her head as she walked to the table. The glass sloshed over the side a bit as she set it down.

"You okay?"

"Fine," she said as she picked up the glass.

"How are you getting home?"

"I have a car."

Tyson's lips pursed. "Yep, but I'm not thinking you should drive it."

"I wasn't going to. I'll go back to my store and stay there for awhile. I'm not stupid. I won't drink and then drive. I won't even text."

He laughed at that. "I didn't mean to get you all worked up over your dad."

She set her glass down and leaned in over the table. "Are you attracted to me?"

His eyes widened, and his face went pale. "Of course. You're a very beautiful woman."

"Why don't you have one?"

"One what?"

"A woman?"

He finished his beer and let out a long breath. "Don't need one."

That was her answer now wasn't it? This date was officially over, she decided as she drank her beer. What a shame too. She was very much hoping to have shown him her very secret tattoos. Now it looked as though they'd simply be awkward around each other and that was a pity, especially since it seemed they'd be attending all the same weddings.

Tyson watched as Pearl's polished demeanor disappeared with each sip she took. How was it he could anger most men and sadden the women? No wonder he didn't need one.

It had been a pain in the ass to drive into town just to be measured for a tuxedo for a wedding and now he was babysitting his cousin's cousin while she wept over her family drama. No thank you.

But he was still sitting there, wasn't he?

Oh, he didn't need a woman, but it didn't mean he didn't enjoy one from time to time. And what wasn't there to enjoy when he looked at Pearl Walker?

It had been hard not to sound like a caveman when she'd asked if he was attracted to her. What living, breathing man wouldn't be?

She was stunning, and he'd been fighting off the signals his body was sending to his brain all afternoon. But watching her skin flush from the alcohol and her infectious good mood slip away, he chose to ignore those incessant signals.

As she finished the last of her third beer, in under an hour, Tyson scooted off his stool and stood.

"C'mon, I'll walk you back to your store."

She lifted her eyes. "Thank you."

With a nod, he held out his hand to her. She took it and stumbled into him as she came off the stool. Once again she was pressed to him, only, this time, she lingered there.

Tyson bit down on the inside of his cheek to keep his mind focused on something other than how she felt there.

Once she found her balance, she looked up at him. "Thank you for being such a gentleman. You're a Morgan, and I'm a Walker. You could just drop me on my ass right here, and no one would think a thing of it."

Tyson took her hands, hoping to steady her, but also to keep her body from his. "I'm not my grandfather, and you're not your father. I don't see where the Morgan and Walker feuds of the past have to work their way into our lives. Not any longer."

A smile formed on her lips. "I think that would be nice. A clean start for this generation."

He chuckled. "Aside from the few black eyes that Eric and I gave each other, yes."

Pearl gathered her purse and flung it over her shoulder. "Thank you for a nice afternoon."

Tyson lifted an eyebrow. "Was it nice? I'm not very good company."

"No, I think you were very good in the company department. I hadn't known I needed it so much."

She took a few steps before stopping, bending down, and removing her high heeled shoes. "Safer this way," she joked as she took his arm and let him walk her down the street.

The street that ran down the old part of town, which was now filled with quaint shops such as Pearl's, had grown busier with pedestrians and cars driving slowly.

Pearl fished for her key in her purse. When she retrieved it, she fumbled to put it into the lock.

"Let me help you," he took the key from her shaking fingers and opened the door.

"Thanks," she said softly as he pushed open the door.

Pearl stumbled inside and giggled to herself. Tyson stood a safe distance at the door. "You promise me you're not going to drive, right?"

"I promise, but you're welcome to stay and make sure I don't go anywhere."

He let out a low growl. "I could just give you a ride home. Then I'd know you weren't going anywhere."

A flash lit in her eyes. "I think maybe that would be the better idea."

Of course, she did. "Well, then get what you need. I'll drive you home. Do you have someone who can drive you back here to get your car tomorrow?"

"I have a whole family at my beck and call."

That she did, no matter how dysfunctional he thought her family was, she had them, and they looked out for each other. He knew that first hand. In the few months in which he'd known he shared blood with Eric Walker, he'd been included in that family. He still wasn't used to it, but it was nice.

"Well then, let's head out," he said before she could lure him any further into the dress shop and make him any more uncomfortable looking at her float from side to side.

Chapter Four

Pickup trucks were supposed to be amazing, Pearl thought as she held on tightly to the door as Tyson drove down the street. His pickup had to be as old as he was. Hadn't she seen him driving a beautiful, brand new truck? Why did he bring the one from the ranch into town?

Because he was a simple man, that was why. He had nothing to prove to anyone she realized very quickly on the quiet drive.

She'd given him the vaguest of directions, yet he'd driven right to her townhouse.

"Can you make it in?" he asked as he pulled to the curb and put the truck in park.

"I'm okay. But would you like to come in for a little bit?" She had to offer. The afternoon wasn't ending the way she'd hoped it would.

"I have things to do. I need to get back to work."

"Right." She fished for her keys again. She should get a clasp for her keys that she could hook into her purse. "Thanks for the company this afternoon. I appreciate it."

"Sure."

"I'll have the tuxes in a few days before the wedding. I'm sure Susan will pick them up and have them for you."

"Works for me."

She was stalling here, and he wasn't buying into it with his short answers.

"Don't forget to talk to Eric's brothers about that bachelor's party."

"Right. I'll do that," he said again with his fingers gripped around the steering wheel.

She had to keep reminding herself that she needed to get out of the damn truck, but she didn't want to. Something was pulling at her, and she wanted to be right there with him. Perhaps that's why she decided to lean across the bench seat, rest her hand on Tyson's cheek, and turn his head until her lips were poised right at his.

She saw the surprise in his wide open eyes as she gently pressed her lips to his.

She lingered only long enough to satisfy that immediate need that buzzed inside of her.

His eyes were still wide when she pulled away. "Thanks again," she said as she opened the door and hurried out of the truck.

Breathe. Breathe. Tyson told himself as he watched Pearl slowly walk to the front door of her house, with her shoes in her hand.

He kept his grip on the steering wheel and did just as he told himself to do as he watched her open the door and disappear inside.

Then, for another moment, he sat there until the tingle she'd left on his lips subsided.

Maybe it would be a good idea to go inside and make sure she was okay. Obviously, she'd had too much to drink to drive home. Perhaps she shouldn't be alone.

Forcing himself to put the truck into drive, he pulled away from the curb. No, she was just fine. He'd already spent too much of his day with the woman and damn it, he had responsibilities. As far as he should be concerned, this had all been a waste of his day.

Pearl watched him drive away from the small window next to the door. What had she done?

She'd acted like an idiot, that's what she'd done. Why in the world had she gotten so worked up over him?

Walking away from the door, she went to the kitchen and pulled a bottle of water out of the refrigerator. Her steady craft beer buzz was wearing off. Maybe she should have just stayed at work and brought her car home later.

Stupidly enough, she'd thought maybe she could convince Tyson to come in. Maybe they could spend some time together.

The very thought had her tensing up. What had driven her to be so lonely that she was hitting on her cousin's family—Lydia's brother? She'd never made a move on the man—never. But today? What was so stellar about today?

Pearl walked to the living room and plopped herself down on the couch. She kicked her bare feet up on the coffee table and rested her head back.

Weddings never used to bother her. She saw happy brides walk in and out of her store all the time. But ever since Susan and Eric got engaged and Bethany and Kent followed right behind, she'd felt the pang of longing for someone.

Always the bridesmaid, never the bride, she thought to herself as she sipped from the bottle of water.

But what did it matter? She was thirty-three years old, had her own place, her own business, and her car was paid off. She didn't need a man for anything—well, except for companionship.

She squeezed the bottle, and it overflowed onto her lap. With a jump, she came off the couch and cursed. "This is stupid. Tyson Morgan isn't worth getting all worked up over," she said aloud as if that would make all the difference.

It was just the moment she reminded herself as she walked to the kitchen for a towel. People she loved were finding happiness and she would too in time. She was caught up in a moment, and that happened sometimes. In two weeks, Susan and Eric would be married. In another two months after that, her sister would marry Kent, and the family wedding craze would be over.

Tyson would be at both weddings. That was fine. Pearl was sure once he got home he'd have forgotten all about her little pity party, or whatever it was, and he'd go on with his life.

They'd be at the same weddings. They'd always have family members in common. No problem, she thought as she dried off her suit. Today was just a strange day, and she was going to write it off like that.

Once she was dry, she went to her purse and pulled her phone out. She hit the contact with her sister Audrey's face on it.

"Hey! Are you working tomorrow?" she asked.

"Yes. I have to go in at nine. Saturdays at the salon pay well, but they suck," Audrey added with a grunt.

"Can you pick me up and take me to my shop?"

"Sure? Jake fixing your car?"

That reminded Pearl that she did need an oil change, and she should call her brother. "No. I had a few beers down the street, and Tyson brought me home."

There was silence on the other end.

Pearl looked at the display on her phone to ensure the connection was still there. "Hello."

"You went out with Tyson Morgan?" There was discomfort in her sister's voice.

"He came and got fitted for his tux. We went down the street for a beer. I had three."

"Those have more alcohol in them you know," she said in her mother-like way.

"I know. That's why he drove me home. So will you pick me up?"

"Sure." She paused for a moment. "Are you seeing him?"

"Tyson?" Pearl swallowed hard. "No. Just a Friday afternoon drink. That's all."

"He's a Morgan," Audrey said again as if she were reminding her what a bad idea it was to have anything to do with him.

Pearl got it, but she didn't buy it. All her sister's accusations were doing were pissing her off. "I got that. I'm a Walker. Oil and Water. One afternoon of drinks. I'm home alone. No reason to get all bent out of shape over this."

"Dad wouldn't like it."

"I don't give a crap about that. Listen, I have to go. Will you be here around eight-thirty?"

"Yes. Please don't make me late."

"I won't," Pearl said, disconnecting the call with a growl.

Tyson drove back to home without even the radio on though he hadn't realized that until he pulled into the large circle drive in front of the house. The sun was low in the sky, giving the fields around the big house a warm glow.

He smiled to himself, this was home and in time, it would all be his. Lydia had no desire to watch it grow. Sure, thanks to his grandfather, the landscape would soon be marred with oil wells. That was cause for another smile. In time, that too would offer more profits for the ranch.

Then again, what good was it if he were the only one there?

His grandfather had a few good years left, but the day would come when he'd pass on. Lydia was all but moved out. Her investments were her way of getting out of the big house and starting her life away from the ranch and the watchful eye of their grandfather.

Tyson put the truck in park, turned off the engine, and climbed out. When he looked toward the door, his grandfather stood there, his arms crossed over his chest in a rigid stance.

"Hey, Grandpa," he said, but his grandfather held his hand up to stop his progress into the house.

"That's a farm truck."

"Yes, sir."

"It belongs out back by the barn. Not in front of the house. And why did you take it into town?"

Tyson ran his hand over the back of his neck. "Susan called and said I had to get to town to get fitted for the wedding. I just took off and headed to town. I'll take the truck and put it away."

"Damn straight you will," his grandfather said as he turned and closed the front door behind him.

Tyson turned, kicked the front tire of the truck, and cursed under his breath. There were days he was very jealous of his sister's forward thinking on getting away from his grandfather.

He climbed back into the truck and drove away from the house. However, moving the truck and parking it elsewhere wasn't giving him any satisfaction. Maybe he'd drive out to Eric's and see what was going on on Walker property. He was fairly sure it had always been more friendly than Morgan property.

There was also that matter of the bachelor party Pearl mentioned. That would be a great reason just to show up. Anything to not face his grandfather for the rest of the evening.

He gripped the steering wheel. It was stupid to be forty-two-years-old and cowering from the man who took care of him his whole life—and lied to him as well.

Either way, he'd probably find Lydia up there riding. And some male bonding with his brother would certainly be more welcomed than being in that huge house alone hiding out in his bedroom like some teenager.

Perhaps male bonding would take the edge off his afternoon with Pearl. That little impromptu kiss of hers seemed to be still lingering on his lips.

Chapter Five

The moment Tyson drove up the dirt road toward Eric's house, he could see his sister out in the pasture. He'd always teased her that she looked like a boy. Her small stature and her short hair never helped her argument that she did not look like a boy.

It brought a smile to his lips to watch her. She looked free—yes, free from everything when she rode. It was a beautiful thing.

He pulled up and parked outside Eric's newly built house. It was hard to believe that only six months ago the house had been a pile of ash and stone and that Eric had almost died in that fire.

He could already see Susan's womanly touches with the flower pots on the front porch. She was good for Eric. Tyson never thought he would have cared, but he did.

Before they knew they were brothers, he and Eric had left a few marks on each other. He supposed that could be what they called making up for their lost childhood together. Though, at the time, Tyson was sure, they were both out to kill the other.

Pulling his truck next to Eric's, he turned off the engine and looked out over the fields in the direction of his home.

He'd ridden to the fence hundreds of times when he was younger. What had been so bad on the other side that his grandfather hadn't wanted him to see? He'd come up with a lot of stories of his own. Though he had never imagined that his biological mother and her other family might be just that close. Who could have known--his grandfather, that's who.

But as far as he knew, the Walkers were bad people and that was that.

Nothing could have been further from the truth.

Susan walked out of the house and waved. He gave her a nod as he climbed out of the truck and shut the door.

She walked toward him. "What are you doing out here?"

"Just taking a drive," he admitted.

"Pearl said you got your tux fitted. Thank you."

He gave her a shrug. "I still don't know why you want me in your wedding."

She reached her hand out and gently placed it on his shoulder. "You are family. Eric's brother. No matter how the past was written, it doesn't have to be the future."

He nodded. "Funny how things happen, huh?"

Her eyes were soft as she looked at him. "Can you stay for dinner?"

"Oh, I don't..."

"Lydia is staying. You might as well stay too."

He looked toward the field where he'd seen his sister. The thought of going home to where his grandfather waited didn't appease him. He shouldn't be a man in his forties and afraid of going home.

"I think dinner would be nice, thank you."

Susan smiled warmly. "I'm glad to hear that. It'll be ready in about forty minutes. Eric, Russ, and Ben are up in the barn."

"I'll head up that way," Tyson said, returning the smile.

He waited until Susan had gone back into the house before starting his walk toward the barn.

There were three trucks parked outside of the barn. His sister's, and the trucks of two of Eric's brothers, Ben and Russell. If he'd been looking for a family bonding moment, it seemed as though he'd certainly chosen one.

The men were fussing over a foal and its mother in one of the stalls. If Tyson were feeling extremely ornery, he'd have called them out on it, as they looked like three women ogling over a new baby. As it was, he was curious too.

"Whatcha got there?" he asked as he approached and all three turned to look at him.

He noted the quick flash of disgust that lit in Russell's eyes before he must have thought better of it. Ben simply gave him a nod, but Eric turned with a smile.

"Hey. Come check her out," he offered.

As Tyson approached the gate, Russell and Ben shifted to one side, as if, perhaps, not to get too close. Okay, so this family bonding thing hadn't crept over into Eric's other brothers—not yet anyway.

He looked into the stall and saw what had captured the men's attention. It was a beautiful new chestnut foal still getting her wobbly legs under her.

"Now that's a sight," he said, his voice cracking under the emotion of seeing them.

It never changed, this was something he'd appreciated since childhood—new life. He could even remember staring at Lydia when she was newborn with the same enthusiasm. At thirteen years old he was old enough to appreciate what a baby meant to the world. He had no idea then how chaotic and strange the future would become, only that he would vow to protect her for the rest of his life.

"Dane bought the mare before he knew he was getting the job in Ohio. I promised to take care of her," Eric said.

"She's a beauty alright. What's her name?"

Ben chuckled, "Fairy Godmother."

Tyson shook his head. "Is there a book on naming horses with funny names?"

Russell lifted his head. "I left a message for Dane to tell him the foal was here and ask what he wanted to name her."

Eric slapped a hand on Russell's shoulder. "Did you give him a suggestion like Cinderella?"

"Is she the one with the Fairy Godmother?"

The four men looked at each other dumbfounded as if they were supposed to know that. Then Tyson supposed, they each wondered how they got to talking about that. They each turned in a different direction and took manly stances as Lydia rode up to the barn.

"What are ya'll doing in here looking guilty?" she asked as she dismounted her horse.

"Talkin' horses," Russell quickly answered as he shoved his hands into his front pockets.

"Could have fooled me." She looked right at Tyson. "What are you doing out here?"

"I suppose the same as you. Staying away from home."

Eric took off his hat and ran his hand over his hair, then replaced it. "You two are pathetic. You should get homes of your own. I'm going back to the house."

Eric walked out, and his brothers followed, but Tyson stayed with his sister as she began to take the bridle off her horse.

"How was your ride?"

"Good," she said as she unfastened the cinch and tossed it up over the saddle. "Why are you staying away from home?"

"Just not in the mood," he said as he reached out and took the saddle off the horse for his sister. "You take this with you?"

"No, I store all my tack here."

He nodded and placed the saddle along the wall with the others. "You still could keep him at home."

She shook her head as she took the blanket off the horse's back. "I'm like you. It's nicer to hide over here."

"Eric was right. We are pathetic."

"You more so than me. I get out and see people. I go to town all the time. I'm here all the time. I have businesses and properties and…"

"I get it," he said picking up a grooming brush. "I went to town today. It wasn't so bad. And I'm here now, and I'm staying for dinner."

He watched her rise from the other side of the horse and look at him though she barely could see over the animal. "You went to town?"

"Got fitted for the tux."

"Good. You saw Pearl then?"

He shrugged as he brushed the horse. "Yeah, I saw her."

"She's single you know," she said as she took the bridle from the horse.

"So what?"

"Just saying."

Tyson lifted the brim of his hat. "We had a drink or two. I think she had three. I took her home after."

His sister appeared next to him. "You went out?"

Tyson held his hands up as if in surrender from her questions. "Just a friendly drink. Thought I needed it after she felt me up with the tape measure and all."

Lydia let out a laugh. "She wasn't feeling you up."

"I beg to differ."

She planted her hands on her hips and looked up at him. "Did you enjoy it at least?"

He winced and lowered the brim of his hat. "Let's just say I was social and leave it at that. She has a reputation that I don't need a part of."

"She had a reputation, and you're no saint." Lydia picked up another brush and moved to the other side of the horse. "She's a very successful business woman, and we're going into business together. She's my new partner."

Tyson rested his hands on the top of the horse's back and looked over to his sister. "How many things are you going to take on?"

"As many as I can. Why sit around and wait for Grandpa to die and inherit what he's made? I want my own. Besides, what happens if he loses it all? You know that gamble with Bryon Walker was part of his doing too. Sure the Walkers were the ones thinking they were going to lose all their land, but it could happen to us. I love him, but it doesn't mean I have to like how he does things."

Tyson eased back and brushed the horse.

His sister was one of the wisest people he knew, and all that wisdom was shoved into a five-foot frame. He chuckled to himself. There was a lot to learn from her.

Being invited to a caterer's house for dinner had its perks. Susan was trying out new recipes, and since she was a vegetarian, she'd invited the others to try meat filled dishes.

Tyson wondered if she'd invited more than Eric's brothers and his sister. There was enough food to feed a small army. No wonder she'd been quick with the invitation.

"I'm going to finalize the cake plans Monday," she said as they all ate and she moved salad around on her plate with her fork. "I like the red icing design, but red icing is nasty."

Lydia looked up. "All of your guests will have red lips."

"I don't want that." She turned to Eric whose head was down as he plowed through his meal. "What do you think?"

He lifted his head slowly. "Whatever, babe."

She chuckled. "That's what I thought."

"I can go with you," Lydia offered. "I'll bet Pearl would have a lot to say about it too."

Just the mention of her name had Tyson dropping his fork and all heads rising to look at him. "Sorry," he said as he went back to his meal.

"She's been great," Susan said finally taking a fork full of lettuce and almost making it to her lips. "She knows everything. I wonder what her wedding would look like?"

"I think simple. She's used to all the fancy stuff. I just think hers would be simple."

Why that made him laugh, he wasn't sure, but again everyone turned to him. "She's not simple. I don't see simple being her wedding design of choice."

A grin formed on his sister's lips. "You know her style now?"

"I'm just saying. That fancy makeup and those expensive shoes. Her jewelry and her hair. That woman isn't simple."

Russell shrugged. "I think she's just professional. She's not too complicated," he defended his cousin.

Tyson took another bite of the meat on his plate. He was in the wrong house to make comments about another Walker. But he kept his conviction. Pearl Walker wasn't simple. She was a whole lot of drama wrapped in a pretty package. He snapped his fork. And he was the man who was thinking way too much about that pretty wrapping.

Chapter Six

It was eight-fifty, and Audrey had promised Pearl she'd be there to pick her up. After all, Audrey had to be to work by nine, so where the hell was she?

The doorbell rang just as she picked up her phone to call her. Throwing her bag over her shoulder and cursing her sister, she pulled open the door.

"You're late! And you told me..." She stopped when she saw Tyson Morgan on her doorstep with his dark eyes wide.

"I'm...sorry?" he said gripping his truck keys in his hand.

"I thought you were my sister. She's supposed to pick me up," Pearl said as her phone rang in her hand. She swiped her finger over the screen and held it to her ear. "Where are you? You said you were picking me up." She groaned as she heard her sister make excuses for forgetting her. Now she couldn't pick her up because she was late for work and in some weird way, it was all Pearl's fault. "Fine. Goodbye." She disconnected the phone with a grunt.

"She's not coming?"

"How'd ya guess?" Pearl shoved the phone into her purse, collected herself, and looked back up at him. "So why are you here?"

"Well, from the sounds of it, I suppose I'm here to give you a ride to your shop."

She narrowed her gaze on him. "Why are you really here?" The alarm on her phone went off, and she pulled it from her purse again and silenced it quickly. "You know I don't care why you're here. I need a ride and if you'd give me one that would be fantastic. I have a bridal showing at nine-thirty, and I haven't even been to the bakery."

Quickly, Pearl pulled the door closed and locked it. She hurried by Tyson and then turned back. "Are you coming?"

"Yup, right behind you."

Pearl was already in the truck when Tyson climbed in and shut the door.

"This is much nicer," she said looking around.

Of course, it was nicer. She'd ridden in the farm truck. That was far from luxurious.

"Thanks. I don't drive it much."

He started the engine, glad that she'd changed the subject from earlier. When she'd asked what he was doing there, Tyson was glad she hadn't waited long for an answer. The truth was, he had no idea what the hell he was doing there.

Something that Lydia had said to him last night seemed to resonate with him. *I get out and see people. I go to town all the time.*

His time in town yesterday hadn't been so bad. A few minutes getting felt up by the grumpy bridal store woman to his right hadn't been horrible. There was beer involved, and that too was good.

Tyson pulled away from the curb. "How can I help you out this morning?"

"You're here to help me?"

Giving a shrug, he rolled down his window. It was getting a little stuffy in the cab of the truck.

"I was in town, thought I'd…" He thought he'd what? Again, he hadn't planned on showing up at her door at nearly nine in the morning. Then he remembered he'd stopped at 7-11 and gotten coffees. "I brought you a coffee," he pointed to the cup holder.

Her eyebrow raised as she studied him. "You came all the way to town to buy me a 7-11 coffee?"

"If you don't make it yourself, it's the best."

She reached for it and eased back. "Thanks."

"You're welcome," he said as he turned at the stoplight. "So, honestly, what can I do to help you this morning?"

"Really? You have time to help me? Because I'll take you up on it. I'm not the kind that…"

"I mean it," he said reaching for his cup.

"Franklin's Bakery has an order for me. I'd be forever indebted to you if you'd pick up my order and bring it back to the store. I have to pull out the dresses I was going to show the bride. Get the room ready. Set out the strawberries and champagne. And…"

"I can do that," he interrupted.

Pearl let out a long sigh and turned toward him. "You didn't come just to make sure I was able to get to work did you?"

Tyson winced. "Maybe. I felt a little guilty that you didn't have your car." *And you haunted my dreams*, he thought to himself. "Needed a few supplies too."

"You came to town two days in a row. That's not normal is it?"

"Nope. Not at all. But Lydia says I need to get out more." And after having sat with his grandfather in silence this morning while he listened to the man chew his toast, he was damn sure he'd be in town more.

Pearl reached over and touched his arm. "Thank you. It means a lot to me."

He felt the sizzle in her touch zap every part of him awake. "It's nothing."

"It is to me."

Pulling the truck up in front of the store he parked. "I'll be back with the order. What am I getting?"

"They have a box of pastries with my name on them. They are already paid for, so you just have to get them. I can call and let them know you're coming."

"Do you need to do that?"

She pursed her lips. "I'll call. Not everyone will believe a Walker sent a Morgan to run their errands."

He nodded and tried not to act or feel as offended as he was.

Pearl gathered her bags and hopped out of the truck. "By the way. I like this truck better. I thought you had a little bit of luxury in your life." She winked and closed the door.

Tyson looked at the truck's interior. Yeah, he'd decked it out when he'd bought it. Leather seats. XM radio. The trim was elegant, and so was the black paint on the outside. It had been his splurge, which was why it spent most of the time in the garage. He didn't want anything to happen to it. The old farm truck was just fine for running around. So why had he pulled this one out this morning?

He waited until she was inside before pulling away.

Pearl watched him drive away and then leaned her back against the door. Her heart was racing so fast she couldn't calm it down to a normal pace.

He'd come for her. He'd come to the door, bought her coffee, and was running errands. How had this happened?

Pushing herself away from the door, she walked to the back of the store and set her bags on the small table in the back room.

She knew how this happened. She'd willed it to happen and then acted on it when she'd measured him for that tux.

Each muscle of his arms had rippled under her fingertips. The massive expansion of his chest had been wrapped in her arms.

No matter what, he'd enjoyed her presence near him too. A woman didn't run her hand down a man's leg and not notice what it did to him.

Pearl fought to catch her breath just thinking about him. And then she'd kissed him.

She had to sit down. What was going to happen? What was going on between them?

Her father wasn't going to like it, and she was damn sure his grandfather would reject the thought of the two of them. But she couldn't think of anything else.

Then reality hit. He was a gentleman who was making sure she could get to work. He'd taken her home when she shouldn't be driving. He bought her coffee and was helping her out. That meant nothing in the realm of falling for her. She'd pawed all over him and then threw herself at him when he'd dropped her off. That hadn't been fair.

Sulking was going to ruin the pristine look she'd put together that morning. There was work to do, so she needed to lift her chin and get to it.

She let the smile form on her lips. Nothing could happen between her and Tyson Morgan. She'd have to deal with that and she would. But it was nice to know that they could be friends, and he'd help her when he could.

The beating of her heart slowed to normal, and she felt the cloud lift from her head. She stood, took the coffee with her, and headed out to sort through the dresses.

***

Tyson stood in line at the bakery while a young boy and his mother tried to choose twelve donuts. How hard could it be, he wondered.

When the door opened again, Tyson turned to see his sister walk in. She smiled at him as though she knew something.

She walked toward him and kissed his cheek. "You're in town again? I saw your truck outside."

"Yeah, so?"

"You don't eat donuts."

He tousled her hair, which she despised. "I'm not here for donuts."

The woman and the boy finally moved, and Tyson approached the counter.

"I'm here to pick up an order for Pearl Walker."

The woman nodded. "She called and said you'd be here. Hey, Lydia."

"Good morning," his sister chirped. Did she know everyone?

"Usual?"

"Please." She turned toward him. "You want anything? My treat?"

"I have coffee in the truck. I have to get these to Pearl."

Her eyes grew wider, and though she wasn't smiling, he knew it was straining to come to the surface.

"You're running errands for her? That's not like you either."

"I'm just helping her out. She got a late start."

Lydia bit down on her bottom lip. "Just what time did you get into town? Why did she get a late start?"

He narrowed his eyes and groaned. "I'm not the reason for her late start. And don't give me crap about helping her out either."

His sister's cheeks had become rosy with whatever she was thinking. "I'm heading that way. I can drop them off for you," she offered and then the smile peeked through.

What the hell did she think she knew? The truth was, she knew nothing.

"That would be great. I got stuff to do at home," he said wiggling out of whatever fantasy his sister had about him and Pearl. That would teach her to stick her nose in things.

"Then why are you here?" The smile was wider now.

"I took her home last night, and I wanted to make sure she had a ride to work. That's all. I'm a gentleman, remember. Mom would kill me otherwise."

The woman handed him the box and he, in turn, handed it to his sister. "Here, you take them to her."

"Are you sure? Did you need to see her?"

He shrugged. "I did what I needed to do," and with that, he left his sister in charge of the box that would have given him five more minutes with Pearl. All the more reason to head back home. Pearl was becoming a distraction.

Chapter Seven

The strawberries were defrosting on a plate. The champagne flutes were set out. And because it was before noon, a glass pitcher of orange juice chilled with the champagne to make mimosas.

Dresses filled the rack in the bride's size and, according to the interview, as to what style suited her.

Pearl had wanted everything to be ready so she could spend just five minutes with Tyson and realize that her giddy buzz from earlier had just been a lack of sleep. That too had been his fault as she'd replayed that kiss in her head all night.

But, she knew what he was like. He was temperamental, unsocial, and a Morgan. That too wasn't fair. Wasn't she considering going into business with a Morgan? There shouldn't even be a pause anymore when she thought about it. Morgans weren't bad people. Her father had been the idiot that caused the problems, and the riff between families started with her grandfather and Tyson's grandfather. It had nothing to do with them.

When the bell over the door rang, her heart rate kicked up again. There was something more to all this, she realized. Otherwise, she wouldn't act so foolish.

She checked herself in the set of mirrors in front of her. Pushing back her shoulders, she gave herself a smile and headed to the front of the store to get the order from Tyson.

Surely the zap of disappointment that filled her showed on her face when she saw Lydia standing in the doorway with the box of pastries she'd sent Tyson for.

"Oh, hi. I wasn't..."

"Expecting me," Lydia set the box on the counter. "I ran into Tyson at the bakery and told him I was coming this way."

"Oh good," she stammered. "He was probably busy."

"I think he was. I think he was busy trying to get your attention." Lydia smiled a brilliant smile.

"I don't know what you're talking about."

Lydia placed her hands on her hips. "I think you do, and I think you owe me an explanation over drinks when you get done. I'm staying in town tonight at my mom's. I'll meet you at Sam's at four. Don't you dare stand me up."

With that, she walked out of the store still grinning.

What was there to explain? Pearl didn't know what was going on herself.

It was nearing four o'clock, and Pearl was ready to lock up when a woman walked into Pearl's store. She had a garment bag in her hand, and mascara streaked down her cheeks. Pearl had seen her share of upset brides before, but something told her this one was different.

"How can I help you?" she asked, but the woman sobbed as she looked up at her.

"I need to have my dress altered. Can you do that here?"

"Yes, I have a woman that does that for me. I send the dresses out and..."

"No. I need it now."

Pearl forced the smile to remain on her face, but inside she wished she'd have locked the door earlier. "When is your wedding?"

That caused the woman to break down in harder sobs that stole her breath and shook her body. Pearl turned to the counter and pulled a few tissues from the box and handed them to her.

"Thank you," she said dabbing at her eyes and nose. "My wedding isn't planned for six more months. I was just planning on coming in next week to look at dresses. Then this morning, well, everything changed." She sucked in a hard breath.

Pearl moved toward her and took the bag. "Why don't we sit down for a moment?"

She escorted her to the small love seat in the viewing area. The room was dark, but the woman seemed comfortable with that.

"Can I get you something to drink?"

The woman shook her head. "I'm fine. I'm so sorry."

"It's okay. Wedding planning can have this effect on people."

She shook her head. "No. I was ready for that. I wasn't ready for the news I got today." Dabbing at her eyes again, she looked up at Pearl. "My father has stage four lung cancer. They don't expect him to live out the next few weeks."

Pearl's heart sank. "I'm so sorry."

"He has to give me away. He has to see me get married." The tears were back. "The dress is my mother's. She's taller than I am, and well, I probably weigh ten pounds more than she did when she was married. But I want to get married in her dress tomorrow."

A battle brewed inside of Pearl. This wasn't her problem. She could sympathize, but...

"Let's look at the dress and see what we can do for you," the words escaped before she could think about it.

The woman's eyes lit up. "You'd do that for me?"

"Every woman deserves to have her father walk her down the aisle if she wants him to. It sounds as though you and your father have a very wonderful relationship."

She nodded. "Oh, we do. I don't know what I'll do when he goes." The tears were back. "He's been my rock all my life. You know?"

Pearl ground her teeth together. No, she didn't know what it was like to have your father be your solid rock. Her father was more the rock that was thrown through someone's window or a rock around your neck when you were drowning.

"I'm going to call my seamstress and see if she's available. I can do a lot of things, but she can do them better."

"I'm Sunshine," the woman held her hand out to Pearl.

"Pearl."

"It's wonderful to meet you."

"Likewise. Sunshine? I don't think I've ever met anyone with that name."

"Oh, yes, it's unique. My daddy named me. It was a gloomy day when I was born, and I brought the sunshine to everyone around."

Now Pearl felt the tug of tears in her throat. "That's precious."

Sunshine laughed. "That's my sister's name."

Of course, it was.

Luck seemed to be on Pearl's side. Emily, her seamstress, was able to join them at the store. Sunshine had taken the dress from the bag, and Emily had swooned at it. Not only had it been her mother's dress, but her grandmother's dress from 1960.

There would need to be many alterations to the dress, but Emily was happy to make them. They had both seen Sunshine's cheeks pink when they began the fitting. It felt good to do something so wonderful for someone.

Pearl knew that she'd be lucky if her father even showed up for her wedding. He'd missed most of her birthday parties as a young girl. He'd even forgotten to attend her high school graduation. At the moment, she couldn't remember where he'd been, but it had been important to him—not to her.

Chances were that if Byron Walker were dying, he'd never even tell Pearl. She'd only learn of his passing when her sister called. He was much closer to Audrey—and that wasn't saying much.

Her sister Bethany had asked him to walk her down the aisle when she married Kent in a few months. He'd taken the time to think about it, which annoyed Pearl, but had agreed. A father shouldn't have to think about it.

Lydia had texted and then called when Pearl hadn't shown up for drinks. Though she had pried for information when Pearl canceled, she made her promise to meet her for coffee tomorrow.

Though she'd grown up with Lydia, she couldn't have called them friends before—from childhood. However, now, she'd refer to her as one of her best friends. It was nice to have a friend she could count on.

Then her mind wandered to Tyson. Could she count on him too—as a friend? Something told her she could.

Sunshine had filled the afternoon with stories about her father and the amazing things he had done. He'd been in the Navy and had met President Reagan when he was younger. She told them of living in Italy and then in Germany. Precious was going to be a doctor one day, and Sunshine was a nanny. She loved to take care of children and be there for them.

Her fiancé was a teacher. A high school history teacher.

Sunshine's eyes lit when she spoke of him. They'd been together for only a year, but she said there was nothing like meeting your soul mate and falling head over heels in love.

They'd been planning on getting married since their fourth date though there was never a need to rush things—until now. She said it had been her fiancé's idea to get married on Sunday. Many of his friends and his family would miss the wedding, but that didn't matter. Knowing that

Sunshine's father walked her down that aisle to him—that's what mattered.

Pearl listened intently and at times found herself swooning over the men in Sunshine's life. What could she possibly say to someone if they ever asked her about her father?

Three hours after Sunshine had walked through the door, she walked out with a wedding dress fit for a princess—and yet unique to her as it was still a beautiful hand-me-down.

Emily had refused payment from Pearl—and Pearl had refused payment from Sunshine. Once in awhile it just felt good to give.

At eight o'clock, Pearl locked the front door to her store and walked to her car. The day had certainly taken a detour from where she'd thought it was going. It had started the moment she'd opened the front door and Tyson Morgan stood there.

His eyes had been dark as he looked at her. All six-foot-four inches of him had seemed small when his shoulders rolled forward as if he were not sure what had drawn him to her house.

It was endearing, she thought.

And then the kiss she'd planted on him the night before wandered into her mind as she opened the door to her car and slid inside. She pressed her lips together.

Had it meant anything to him? Or had he written it off as something Pearl Walker just did?

As she started the car, a sudden sea of loneliness washed over her. She'd missed drinks with Lydia. After work, Audrey was usually too tired to want to do anything—not that Pearl had asked too many times.

She sighed. Was that all she could think about when it came to keeping company?

Susan had moved out to Eric's and Bethany and Kent—well they didn't need her sad company.

Sunshine crossed her mind. Certainly she was probably with family. They were planning a wedding for tomorrow.

At that moment, Pearl knew she needed her mother to take away this loneliness that filled her heart at that moment. Even that might be a stretch, but she had to try. She just didn't want to go home and be alone.

Chapter Eight

When Cassandra Walker opened the door, a large glass of wine in her hand, her face didn't exactly register excitement seeing Pearl standing on the porch. Concern shadowed her gaze before a smile finally surfaced on her lips.

"Is everything okay? You didn't call first. Is your sister okay? Are you sick?"

"I'm fine, Mom. Can I come in?"

"Oh, yes." Her mother stepped back, and Pearl walked through the door.

Any other child might have an open invitation into their parents' houses, but Pearl still knocked on the door as if she were a typical guest. She didn't even have a key.

"I'm having a glass of wine. Would you like one?"

Pearl considered it for a moment but decided against it. "I'll get myself a glass of water if that's okay."

"Of course."

Pearl walked to the kitchen, her mother close behind. She opened the cupboard, which housed only four glasses, four plates, and an array of tea cups.

She took a glass and moved to the refrigerator to use the water dispenser. All the while her mother watched her as if she might put something in the wrong place.

"You're sure everything is okay?" Her mother's voice had softened to a warm level. Pearl had been sure it would come. Her mother had to be eased into everything. As horrible as it might be, she could sometimes understand why her father felt the need to stray during their marriage.

"I just had a strange day. I wanted a little company."

That moved her mother. She could see the glistening in her eyes. "That's very sweet that you came by."

"Can we sit?" Pearl asked motioning to the kitchen table.

"Yes. Please."

Pearl pulled out a chair and waited for her mother to do the same before she sat down.

"A woman came into the store just as I was getting ready to close," she began her story. If she didn't just dive in, the awkwardness of working her way into the conversation might take an hour. "She had been planning on getting married in six months, but she had just learned that her father had stage four lung cancer and might not live but a few weeks. She wanted her dress altered so she could get married tomorrow and he could walk her down the aisle."

Her mother nodded slowly as if she were trying to figure out the meaning of her story. "Did she buy the dress from you?"

"No. It was a hand-me-down dress she needed to be altered."

"She thought you could alter a wedding dress over night? I don't understand people."

Pearl winced. No, she most certainly didn't understand people.

"It wasn't a problem. It was sweet that they wanted to get married so he could be there. She's very close to her father." It nearly hurt to say that.

"I wonder where they will get married. Churches are busy on Sundays."

Pearl stared at her mother. If it weren't a damning phrase to herself, she'd label her mother a typical dumb blonde.

She watched as her mother nearly downed the glass of wine she'd been carrying around. How in the world had she thought this was going to be comforting?

The thought then zipped into her head that she should have driven all the way out to her Aunt Glenda's house. Glenda Walker was the epitome of a caring mother. Next time she'd consider that. The longer drive would be nothing compared to the discomfort she was feeling in her mother's house.

Pearl decided this would be an opportunity to soften the conversation by including her mother—that usually seemed to work.

"I'm sure they'll work her in, or she'll get married at her house or something. But it got me thinking about how devastating it would be to lose a parent—or expect to lose one."

Her mother nodded. "I can't imagine my mother or father dying," she said. "Daddy set up that trust fund all those years ago. I don't know if your grandmother would know how it works."

And at that moment, Pearl was sure she'd been adopted. Seriously, how could her mother be so shallow?

"I'm sure grandma would figure it out." She drank down the water in her glass. "Would you like this in the dishwasher?"

Her mother looked perplexed. "Yes. Alexa will find it there when she comes to clean."

"Alexa?"

"My housekeeper," she said as if she'd had the same conversation with Pearl a hundred times. Yet Pearl had never heard of Alexa.

"Why do you have a housekeeper?"

"Don't you?" She looked offended.

"No. I clean the store and my house." Pearl stood, and her mother followed. "Thanks for letting me stop by."

"Oh, call ahead next time. I must look a fright," she said, leaning in to kiss Pearl on each cheek, but at a distance.

"I will."

Pearl left her mother's house, and once she was only a block away, the tears began to stream down her cheeks. She understood that her father was a mess of a man. And the older she got, she understood her mother was a perfect match for him.

Her brothers' mother, Naomi, wasn't quite the wreck of a woman Pearl's mother was. Perhaps out of the three women her father had children with, Naomi was the sanest.

Was it too much to wish that she'd been born on the other side of the Walker family?

Even though Eric wasn't Glenda's blood son, she treated him as she treated her other four boys. They were loved and cared for. She was concerned for them, and their future and she wasn't afraid to show them how much she loved them— even as adults.

Glenda doted on her husband, Everett. She had even become a very intricate part of Susan's catering company, and Susan had yet to marry her son.

Even as a child, Pearl remembered wishing that she lived out in the house on the Walker land. A part of her felt as though she belonged there.

But it was more than just a name. It was a feeling when she was at the house.

Glenda baked cookies. Her mother drank wine. Glenda didn't have any girls, so when Pearl and Audrey were around, they'd even play dress-up. Again, her mother drank her wine.

Glenda had made a cake, salad, and bought a gift when Pearl graduated from high school. Her father had forgotten to show up, and her mother drank wine.

Maybe it wasn't too late to ask to be adopted.

The thought made her laugh and she desperately needed to laugh.

By the time she'd returned home the tears had dried. There was a reason she lived alone in town and owned her own business. It proved that she could be her own person and didn't need the Walker name or her parents to help her with anything.

Soon, she and Lydia would be business partners, and it would be one more notch in her success belt. They were going to pool their resources and buy a venue that would house all elements of bridal planning. There would be a kitchen for Susan to work out of. Bethany had agreed to give floral design a try. There was a banquet hall where they could have receptions and a quaint garden where they could have wedding ceremonies.

Pearl had been in touch with a photographer friend who was interested in renting a space as well. The possibilities were limitless and the more she thought about it, the giddier she became. Timing was just right too. Her lease on her shop was up, and she hadn't renewed it because Lydia said nothing could go wrong. Pearl felt that in her heart too. This was the time to change everything.

As she put the car in park outside her house, she let out a long cleansing breath. Though her mind zipped about with possibilities for her and Lydia, her body was exhausted. She was ready to rest her head on her pillow and forget the day.

But as she stepped out of the car and locked the doors, she thought about Sunshine walking into her store. A pang of jealousy ripped right through her, stealing the momentary delight she'd just had envisioning the future.

It was wrong to envy Sunshine, but she couldn't help it.

Pearl realized that she wanted to feel as connected to her family, as Sunshine was to hers, that to lose one of them would shatter her. And wouldn't it be nice to be loved enough by someone, that they'd marry you the next day if you wanted to?

Sunshine was a very lucky woman, and she knew it too.

The weight of the day landed on Pearl's shoulders. She'd never have a relationship with her parents like Sunshine had with hers. Not everyone was meant to, she supposed. And she was damn sure no man would ever want to marry her. Walker women were messes.

With that sad thought, she unlocked the front door to her quiet and dark house.

***

Tyson sat on the tailgate of the farm pickup and watched the sunrise with a mug of coffee in his hands. He'd been getting up long before the rooster for most of his life, and his payment had been watching sunrises.

There was something tranquil in watching a dark sky lighten and then glow in bright hues of reds, oranges, and yellows. The sound of footsteps drew his attention away from the glorious painting happening before him.

The approaching figure didn't startle him. It had grown to be an often event that his sister walked up on him and shared in the silent glory with him.

"I thought you were in town at Mom's."

She cradled a mug in her hands. As she neared the truck, she handed him the mug and in one quick jump, she landed next to him on the tailgate. Taking her mug, she sipped the coffee that steamed.

"I was. Couldn't relax. Couldn't sleep. So I drove back out here very, very, early this morning," she groaned.

"I never heard you."

"I said it was early."

Tyson watched as the grand ball of yellow began to encompass the horizon. Soon the sky would just be light, and the magnificent color celebration would be over. Usually, he'd watch and talk later, but he wondered what had his sister so tense.

"What's on your mind?"

She sipped her coffee again as if she were gathering her thoughts. "The new property we're acquiring."

It was nature to shake his head. "This is the one you and Pearl are buying?"

She nodded. "It's more than just a property. It would be a wedding mecca."

He couldn't help but chuckle. "A mecca?"

"Yeah," she said on an optimistic sigh. But when she didn't say anything else he knew there was something about this mecca that wasn't sitting right with his sister.

"And what's wrong with it?"

She looked up at him. Her dark eyes narrowed on him, and she raked her hand through her short crop of hair. "You just assume?"

"You have tells. What's up?"

"We have tenants already. So it'll have income right off. But it looks like there's going to need to be more work done to it than we'd expected. It's going to eat up the budget faster than anticipated."

"So maybe it's not the right time to buy."

She shook her head. "I can't let this go. Do you know what the wedding industry brings in every year?"

"Do you?"

She gave him a punch on the arm, then strangled her coffee mug with both hands. "People will pay nearly ten thousand dollars for a wedding. Sometimes more. If you can get them to drop all ten thousand in one place, you're golden."

"And then you hope they divorce and do it all over again?"

She shrugged. "Some will."

"Yep, doesn't even sound like something to be optimistic about." He gave her a nudge. "So what's the real problem?"

"Money," she answered quickly.

"Ask Grandpa," he was quick with his answer.

She let out a threatened gasp. "No. Never. Not in a million years. I'll figure it out."

"Do you need another loan?"

"I'm too stretched out on loans, and all of Mom's assets are in the Garden Room."

"So you bought into the Garden Room, that restaurant we had dinner in a few months back..."

"I sold that share."

"Okay," he said grinning at her business sense. "Now this? What kind of money do you need?"

She winced. "More than Pearl and I have."

"And you can't ask her dad for money. He owes everyone else."

She nodded. "We need another partner."

Tyson rubbed the stubble on his chin. "What about Bethany? Doesn't she..."

"She has nothing. She's still paying off some of her mom's debts."

"That sucks."

"We either find another investor or we have to back out. That's it. But we have to do it and get going in the next two months if we commit. Pearl's lease is up then, and she held off on signing an extension." Now she lifted her eyes up to him in a near plea. "We need another partner."

He knew where she was going with this, and he wasn't sure he was interested. They each had a trust fund set up from their father's inheritance. Their mother had invested most of her share of his inheritance in businesses that were thriving. But even thriving businesses still needed a reserve, he understood that.

Tyson had always been very frugal with his money. In fact, he lived on the ranch free and clear. He made a living—

a good living. The only expense at forty-two years old was the upkeep on his truck, which he rarely drove.

That gnawed at him more than he thought it should. No man of his age should have nothing, and he had nothing.

"What does this partner have to do?" he asked, keeping his eyes on the sun that was now bright on the horizon.

He caught sight of the smile Lydia tucked in which had crept up on her lips when he asked. "They could be a silent partner. You know, they'd have no dealings in the day to to day operations, but when profit was made, they'd make their money back and some."

"You want me to invest in this, don't you?"

The smile fully surfaced now. "You're our only hope right now. Pearl believes in this—in me. She's taking a chance, and I have to make it work for her or she could lose everything."

Tyson finished his coffee, which had gone cold and bitter. "Why would she do that? Why partner up with you? You weren't that close growing up."

"But we are now. And she's a business woman. I'm a business woman. It doesn't matter that we didn't run in the same crowd years ago. She's not who she was, and neither am I."

He nodded. He wasn't sure if that was a good thing or a bad thing that Pearl might be different. The old Pearl had an edge that guaranteed no one would mess with her. Did business-minded Pearl, in her fancy clothes, still have that edge?

"Don't you think you should discuss my involvement with Pearl? She doesn't know me." He narrowed his gaze on his sister. "Does she even know that you need more money?"

Lydia crinkled up her nose. "She knows we need help."

"If I decide to do this don't you think you'd better discuss it with her first?"

That had her wincing. "I was hoping you'd discuss it with her."

"Me?" His voice rose into an unfamiliar octave. "This is your idea."

"And you seem to have some connection with her."

His muscles tensed. "She felt me up for a tux."

That sent his sister into a bout of laughter. "And you enjoyed every moment of it so don't play that game." When the humor died down, she looked him square in the eye. "Please. Go to town. Look at the place. Drop in and talk to Pearl. Me asking her or telling her won't be the same. She has to know that anyone involved has her best interest at heart. And yes, I'll talk to her. But you check it out first."

Tyson bit the side of his cheek as his head spun. He'd never let his sister down. "You knew I'd give you the money if you asked, didn't you?"

"I hoped you would."

"I haven't said yes yet."

"Yet."

He let out a growl. "Where is the building and where do I find Pearl Walker on a Sunday?"

Chapter Nine

Music played in the kitchen as Pearl cracked eggs into a bowl. Lazy Sunday mornings were something she lived for.

Her hair was piled in a mess atop her head. She had on a pair of bunny slippers which Audrey had given her for Christmas one year. The shorts she'd worn to bed were comfy, and so was the thin T-shirt that clung to her body. Sundays at home there was no need for a bra.

The thought made her do a little dance as she picked up the fork and beat the eggs that would eventually make a delicious omelet.

Coffee brewed in the pot to her right and bacon sizzled on a pan in the oven. It had five more minutes to cook and then she'd begin her omelet. Susan had taught her that timing was everything when bringing a meal together. Pearl suffered from timing in the kitchen, but she was feeling optimistic that everything was going to turn out just right.

She had just enough time to walk out and get the Sunday paper off of her porch. It was only good for all the ads, she thought. Often she gave the rest of it to her neighbor who had a kid with a hamster.

Pearl pulled open the door, already in a slight bend ready to pick up the paper when she noticed a pair of very worn boots standing on her porch.

Slowly she lifted her eyes from the boots up the legs and body to the face of one very surprised Tyson Morgan.

In his hand, he held the newspaper she'd come to retrieve.

It didn't go unnoticed that he was about to knock, but now was scanning a look over her in her short pajama pants, braless T-shirt, and her hair piled high on her head.

"Mornin'," his voice croaked as he spoke.

"Hi," her breath caught as she replied.

"I was just about to knock."

"I see that."

"Here's your paper," he said handing it to her.

Quickly she pulled it from his hands and held it to her chest. Chances were he hadn't missed the firming of her nipples against the thin fabric when she'd seen him.

"What are you doing here?"

Tyson scratched the whiskers on his cheek and then adjusted the brim of his baseball cap.

"Right. Um…" He tucked his hands into the front pockets of his jeans. "Lydia sent me to talk to you. It's business. About your business. The one you're going into with her."

"The bridal mecca?"

He chuckled. "Yup. That one."

"Are you getting married?" she asked and then hoped he didn't say yes. She wasn't sure she could handle that right now.

"No. No." His answer was firm. "Can I come in?"

Pearl stared at him. Did she want him in her house? Yes, she did.

"I have coffee and bacon. I was just about to whip up an omelet. Would you like some?"

His lips tightened as if he were giving it some thought, but didn't want to impose. But then his eyes lit. "I would. Do you mind?"

"I offered, didn't I?"

So, she wasn't a morning person. Twice she'd found him on her doorstep and twice she might not have been so glad to see him.

Pearl stepped back and Tyson stepped inside. He'd never been inside of her house, and now that he was there he felt a bit odd about it.

Having seen the girlie interior of her store, he might have thought her house would be spotless and white. That surely wasn't the case.

She wasn't neat and tidy, but she wasn't messy either. Her purse sat open on a chair in the living room. Shoes were tossed aside by the door. A blanket she might have wrapped herself in while watching TV was thrown on the couch and a forgotten plate and glass sat on the coffee table.

It brought a bit of pure joy to his heart to see this side of her.

"Do you want anything in your coffee?" Pearl asked from the kitchen.

He hadn't even noticed she walked past him. "No. Just black."

Walking through the doorway to the kitchen, he watched as she turned with a mug in her hand. She wasn't covering herself up now, and there wasn't much left to the imagination.

Tyson swallowed hard and willed every manly part of him to behave.

She was a mess. Her hair piled on her head and a smudge of makeup under her eyes. Nothing should have been stirring in him, but damn he couldn't help it. Her disheveled look didn't distract from her beauty.

Taking the mug from her, he looked down at the floor. "Thanks."

"I'm going to go change. The bacon has a few more minutes. When the timer goes off, just pull it out. There are oven mitts on the counter."

He nodded, looking into his coffee now as she scurried away. However, he did manage to take a look over the edge of the mug as he sipped and caught her walking out the door. She sure had an excellent body.

When the timer buzzed, Tyson set his coffee down and pulled the tray of bacon from the oven. She was a crispy bacon kind of person. He liked it a little floppy.

Setting the tray down on the trivet on the counter, he noticed she'd already started beating the eggs for the omelet she'd said she was going to have. Obviously, she hadn't been expecting a guest. It wouldn't hurt to add a few more eggs he thought.

With a careful hand, he picked up two more eggs and cracked them into the bowl. After discarding the shells, he went to work. His mother always added a little bit of milk to the mix. He pulled open the refrigerator and found a nearly empty quart of milk, which was set to expire at the end of the day.

He added a drop of milk and turned on the burner on the stove.

Pearl had already set out her cheese and the few items she was planning to put into the omelet. There was no reason to assume she wasn't going to use everything. He'd just make one big omelet, and they could split it.

He looked at the bag of cheese. It too looked as though it might be on its last day and there wasn't much of it. Maybe he'd let her have most of the omelet.

Pearl could smell the bacon. He'd taken it from the oven. That was good. Now she could smell something else.

Quickly she finished with the mascara she'd started to put on and gave herself one more look in the mirror.

Aside from not having had a shower, she thought she looked pretty good.

She'd pulled her hair back in a ponytail, washed her face, and added some mascara and tint to her lips. The yoga pants she'd chosen were brand new, so they looked nice. Most important was the bra she'd put on. She couldn't believe he'd seen her without one. Even dressed, no woman should let a man see her braless unless he was the one that took it off of her.

The tank top she'd chosen wasn't as casual as the yoga pants, but she was attracted to the man. She did want to entice and impress him a little.

Her cheeks heated. She'd found him on her front porch twice in two days. Perhaps that was a sign that she had enticed him. Was there a genuine interest there?

Pearl had brushed her teeth, but for good measure, she gargled some mouthwash. Breakfast was probably going to taste funny now, but it was worth it.

As she descended the stairs, she could hear dishes rattle and the sound of the pan on the stove. When she turned the corner, she could admit she was genuinely impressed.

"You finished breakfast?"

He turned, and she noticed his eyes widen as he took her in. Quickly he went back to his task. "Yeah. Thought I could be helpful."

"Thank you," she said with a sultry tone in her voice that she hadn't planned. "I'll get some forks."

She eased up next to him and pulled open the silverware drawer. He was close now. So close she could feel the heat from his body. Inhaling, she caught the scent of his soap on his skin. It was nice. Thoughts of having wrapped her arms around him while she measured him sent a tingle down up her spine.

It was enough to have her shake away the sizzle that traveled through her. Though she must have forgotten, he was right behind her, because she backed right into him, causing him to lift his hands to her waist to steady her.

"Everything okay?"

Pearl turned quickly in his arms before he could remove his hands completely. "Everything is perfect."

The kitchen wasn't very big, and usually, that bothered her. Today, however, she was grateful that they were nearly pinned against the counter in the small space.

With a fork in each hand, she let her body press up against his. His hands still held her in place.

Tyson's eyes had gone dark.

He moved his gaze from her eyes to her lips and back again. "You have a tattoo on your back," he said, his voice raspy.

Pearl blinked slowly. "You saw it?"

"Your shirt wasn't very long." His Adam's apple bobbed in his throat as he swallowed. "Your shorts weren't very—high on your waist." His breath had grown heavy.

The air in the kitchen became thick and hot. "I hadn't expected company," she said easing against him as his fingers dug into the skin on her hips though the thin fabric of the yoga pants. "How much of it did you see?"

She felt his thumb making a small circle on her hip bone, and it was sending wild signals to all parts of her body. Signals she wasn't sure she could continue to ignore.

"There were wings," he said as he stepped in closer to her and her back pushed up against the kitchen counter. "Butterfly or angel?"

He lowered his face so that their mouths were a breath apart. Pearl wrapped her arms around his neck as they hovered close.

Her mouth had gone dry, but she managed, "Perhaps you should look for yourself."

Those must have been the words that snapped his control. Tyson's mouth came down on hers with a fury, and she accepted. Their lips parted ways as their tongues fought to dance and their bodies pressed together.

Pearl dropped the damn forks on the ground and pulled Tyson's hat off, dropping it as well. She wanted to run her fingers through the short crop of hair he always kept hidden.

His hands left her hips and skirted just under her T-shirt so that they were on her skin. She sucked in a breath with the kiss that consumed her.

Pearl lifted a leg around Tyson's hips, and he took the invitation to lift her to the counter where she wrapped both legs around him and pulled him in closer.

Breath had to be fought for. Heat now came from both the stove and their bodies.

She realized they'd left the pan cooking. "The eggs," she managed as his kiss swallowed up her voice.

Tyson pulled back. "Damn it." He broke from her for a moment and removed the pan from the burner. The eggs were burnt.

Just as quickly, he turned off the stove and moved back to her, gathering her up around him and carrying her away from the kitchen.

She pressed her lips to the throbbing vein on his neck, and he moaned as he took her to the living room and deposited her on the couch with a thud.

"Ow," she groaned.

"Sorry," he said as he lowered himself down on her and she tangled herself around him again.

Tyson didn't know what was going to happen, but dear God, he just didn't care. Every part of him had stiffened the moment he saw her in that thin T-shirt. He couldn't be held responsible for this.

This wasn't just his masculine needs taking over. She was as fueled up as he was.

They were mature adults. Something like this was bound to happen anyway, right? They'd been skirting around it for months at dinners and parties. After she'd felt him up while she measured him, it had only added fuel to the fire that had been simmering.

She ran her hands over his chest, and he was sure he'd growled an inhuman sound. Then she bit his lip, and that only caused him to grind his body closer to her.

With her hands flat against his chest, she pushed him back, but her sapphire blue eyes remained locked on his.

He watched, with great appreciation, as she lifted the T-shirt off her body, exposing her pale, soft skin for him to feast on.

His eyes moved directly to the tattoo she had on her rib cage.

"Chinese?" His breath could hardly carry the words.

She nodded. "Breath of life."

"Sexy," he said as he ran his fingers over the ink and she arched beneath him.

God, he'd never wanted anyone as much as he wanted her right that moment. He was so thankful his sister talked him into driving to town to speak to her.

Talk to her. He wasn't supposed to be doing this. There was supposed to be business going on.

Pearl reached up and wrapped her arms around his neck, pulling him back down atop of her. Business was going to have to wait. They were working on another kind of partnership.

Chapter Ten

It wasn't Tyson's style to act on impulse, but something about Pearl Walker had him forgetting all about that. If he were coherent enough, he'd be thinking that beneath him, half dressed, was his brother's cousin. He'd be damning himself for letting a simple gesture escalate to this. He'd be fighting harder so that his sister didn't get hurt in the crossfire.

But there was no stopping him. Her fingers were working the snaps on his shirt and a moment later her hands were on his skin.

God was going to strike him down—and damn, it would be worth it.

Pearl's chest heaved under his as she pushed away his shirt. She nipped at his lip, and he was sure the maddening pace of his heart meant it was going to explode.

The rush of blood nearly deafened him. Then there was the steady knocking of his heart in his ears. No—that wasn't his heart.

Pearl pulled her lips from his. "Someone's here."

He kept still. "Do we just wait for them to go away?"

Her eyes fixed on his, and she nodded. But the knocking continued. Then he heard the one voice that ripped the moment from them.

"Tyson, I see your car. I know you're in there. What are you two doing? Open the door," Lydia's plea continued with more persistent knocking.

In one fluid motion, they were both off the couch and frantically dressing.

"Did you know she was coming over?" he asked.

"No. Did you?"

"No. She sent me. Why would she follow me?"

"Why did she send you?"

He realized they never had talked about his reason for being there. Lust seemed to have gotten in the way.

"You need a partner."

"I have one," she said quickly raking her fingers through her hair and tying it back up on the top of her head.

"No, Lydia says you need another one. You need more money for the building."

"She should have told me that," she whispered as she headed for the door.

"I was here to tell you that."

"So what do you have to do with it?"

"I'm your partner," he managed before she pulled open the door and his sister stood there staring at both of them.

"Oh, good. You're both here. Are you burning something?" she asked as she stepped inside. "Anyway, did you talk? Are we cool?"

Tyson ran his hand over his head and realized his hat was on the kitchen floor. Seriously, it had to be very obvious what they'd been doing.

"We didn't get down to the specifics quite yet. I didn't get here too long ago."

Her eyes widened. "Oh, I thought you came straight here."

He winced and hoped she didn't notice it. "I was just telling her how you said that you needed another partner."

Lydia smiled that energetic smile that could quickly become contagious.

"Pearl, I thought it would be better if he talked to you about his partnership. We could use more funding, and he's willing."

Tyson pursed his lips. He didn't quite remember telling her he'd do it, but that was how his sister worked. She spun things to benefit her—and it usually worked.

Pearl smiled, but it was obviously forced. "We hadn't gotten to that quite yet." She shifted him a glance then turned toward Lydia. "I ruined my breakfast when I answered the door. What do you say we all go out, and we can discuss this new partnership?" Her words were strained, but by Lydia's reaction, she hadn't noticed.

"I'd love that. Oh, there's a new brunch menu at Toddy's. What do you say?"

They both looked at Tyson as if he were the deciding party. "Fine."

"If you don't mind, I'm going to head upstairs and take a very quick shower. I wasn't quite ready to receive visitors this morning. I'll only be a few minutes. Help yourself to coffee," Pearl added as she headed for the stairs.

When she'd disappeared, Tyson walked toward the kitchen, Lydia close in tow. He picked up his hat from the floor, and the two dropped forks. He tossed the forks in the sink and placed his hat on his head when Lydia hauled off and punched him in the arm.

He wasn't sure if it hurt or if he was simply shocked.

"What in the hell was that for?"

Her eyes were narrowly staring at him, and her lips were in a tight line. "What are you doing?"

"I was going to get coffee."

"That's not what I mean, and you know it." She wound to hit him again, but this time, he moved out of her way.

"You're crazy."

"You're making a move on Pearl."

"I am not," he said, fully convinced that since she was the one that took her shirt off, she'd made the first move.

"You can't sleep with her."

"I didn't."

"You're thinking about doing it."

"I'm a man. Of course, I'd think about it."

He flinched when she reached out to touch his arm. "Tyson…"

There was a tone—a damn maternal tone. He was a forty-two-year-old man. He should be able to carry on with anyone he chose.

"Lydia, it's not like that."

She pulled back and crossed her arms in front of her. "Really? That's not how it looks."

What was he supposed to say to that? If she'd walked right in she'd have gotten one hell of a show.

Tyson let out a long breath. "I like her. Okay? Fine, I've said it. I like her."

"I need this business to work."

"And it can't work if I'm seeing her?"

Her eyes widened. "I knew it."

He held his hands up in surrender. "Stop. You don't know anything."

"Every time Mom gets personally involved with a business partner, something goes wrong. You're going to mess this all up."

"Okay then, I don't want anything to do with it."

"You have to. I need you to be part of this."

Tyson lifted off his cap and ran his hand over his hair. "This is very confusing to me," he said as he adjusted the cap back low over his forehead. "I'll tell you what. Find another partner. I like her."

"There is no one else. No one I trust enough."

He bit down hard, so hard his jaw popped. Family was more important than any amount of money or any degree of lust. He knew that. He abided by that. And right now it really sucked.

Pulling his keys from his pocket, he leaned in and kissed his sister on the cheek. "Tell Pearl I'm sorry I won't be joining you."

Tyson started for the door with Lydia following. "Where are you going?"

"You made it very clear I can't help you and have her. I think you're wrong, but you two had this arrangement first. I'll always choose you, Lydia. You're my family, my blood, my sister."

Pearl walked down the stairs and straight to the kitchen to find Lydia standing there alone.

"I heard the door."

Lydia wrinkled up her nose and closed her eyes tight before opening them and looking at Pearl. "Tyson left. I think I upset him."

Trying to make it seem as if it didn't matter, she simply nodded. "Okay, then just you and I for brunch?"

"You're not mad?"

"Mad that you pissed off your brother? No, should I be?" She gathered her purse off the kitchen table. "Do you want to drive or shall I?"

Lydia studied her for a moment. "You can drive. We can head over to the new building and look at it too. Sometimes just looking at it makes my day better."

"That sounds like a plan."

Pearl and Lydia walked to the front door, and Pearl locked it behind them.

What had happened while she was in the shower, she wondered. Perhaps it was good that Lydia arrived when she had. Pearl's family was temperamental enough. Did she really need a man in her life that was the same? After all, if he'd walked out because of some little disagreement with his sister, he wasn't too open to others then.

All the better.

Right now her focus needed to be on her business. This venture with Lydia had to work out, or Pearl could lose everything, and she wasn't willing to risk that, not even over a man that made her melt into a pile of goo as Tyson Morgan did.

Chapter Eleven

Brunch was excellent. Lydia filled the entire morning with talk of exciting plans for their business. She'd been in contact with a woman named Gia Gallo, who owned a small store not far from Pearl's bridal store.

"She's this tiny Italian woman who sells gifts from Italy. She remembered seeing Bethany in her store before when I mentioned that I knew her."

Pearl lifted a bite of eggs to her lips. "You were name dropping?"

"Seriously, when you can, you do."

Pearl wasn't sure Bethany would like that much, but she wasn't going to say anything. Lydia's hands flew about as she told her that Gia had agreed to open her location in their building.

"So not a wedding mecca anymore?" Pearl asked.

"She has beautiful lace from Venice. Something old and blue?"

"That's all?"

Lydia laughed. "No. That's not all. She comes with rent."

Pearl had to look at it, in the same way, Lydia did. It was a business. They were doing this to make money and a lot of it.

However, her mind wasn't focused on the business at hand at all. It was wandering off to Tyson and wondering why he'd left without another word.

She continued to listen to Lydia talk about her plans all the while wondering if Tyson would show up on her front stop for a third time tomorrow.

~*~

Lydia's truck pulled up the drive toward the Walker's barn. Right on time, Tyson thought as he pulled a beer from the cooler he had on the tailgate of his truck.

He watched as his sister parked and climbed out of her truck, an enormous smile on her face.

"What are you doing here?" she asked as she walked toward him.

"Waiting for you." He held out the beer to her, and she took it. "Still can't convince you to to keep your horse in our barn?"

She laughed as she twisted the cap off the bottle. "He likes it here better."

At that moment, Tyson couldn't blame the horse, or his sister, for spending all their time there. He found he tended to like it better too.

Tyson reached into the pocket of his shirt and handed his sister the folded piece of paper he'd tucked there. "This is for you."

Lydia took it from him and opened it slowly. He watched her eyes widen and tears quickly well up in them. "Tyson, this is a lot of money," she said looking back down at the check he'd handed her.

"Is it enough?"

"It's more than enough. We didn't need…"

"Take it. I believe in what you're building. I think it will do well for you. Susan's already been talking about the kitchen she'll be able to cater out of."

Lydia tucked the check into her pocket and held her bottle up to his. "To partnership," she said

He tapped his bottle to her. "Silent partnerships."

Tyson lifted his bottle to his lips, but Lydia lowered hers. "I'm sorry about everything I said to you today about Pearl. I had no right to…"

"You were right. We're partners now. All three of us. There can be no *getting involved* with partners."

She took a breath to speak again, but Susan was running up the road toward them waving. Tyson chuckled. "She's been waiting for you. Some wedding planning something. It's way out of my league."

Lydia moved in and kissed him on the cheek. "Thank you for this. You won't regret it," she said as she turned and walked toward Susan.

He took a pull from his beer. He'd never regret giving her his money, even down to his last penny. But he wasn't so sure about the rest of it. Hormones and a beautiful woman might have put him in the position he'd found himself in that morning. He thought about that position—her beneath him, skin to skin. Taking another pull from his beer, he let the heat of it settle in his belly. But there was more.

He tipped his head back and let the small breeze drift over him. There was something more than just heat and attraction between him and Pearl, he thought.

For the past few months, since Tyson and Eric had been bonding as brothers, Tyson had been bonding with all members of the Walker family and Pearl, of course, had caught his eye.

Oh, he'd played it cool. He'd taken every dinner invitation extended his way—as a group. When Eric and Susan had moved back into the house and hosted a party, he'd lurked in corners all night and stole moments of conversation with Pearl here and there. And hadn't she seemed always to have been here and there—near him?

He drank from the bottle again.

It had been building. Who could blame them for what had happened?

Tyson let out a long ragged breath as he set the empty bottle in the bed of the truck, turned, and pushed the tailgate back up. Whatever there might have been between them, it was over before it started. They were business partners now and just as Lydia had said, there was no room in business for—well, whatever it might have been.

He walked around the truck and pulled open the door. It was time to head home and dive back into life as he knew it. Susan and Eric's wedding was only two weeks away. He supposed he'd see her then. Things would have died down between them by then and everything would be normal again. What a shame, he thought as he started the engine and gripped the steering wheel. He never did get to see that tattoo on her back.

~*~

The alarm on the nightstand to her right, buzzed and rattled. Pearl turned and slapped her hand down over the top of it just as her cell phone buzzed next to it.

She fumbled for the phone and turned off the secondary alarm.

It was stupid she thought, now laying there staring at the ceiling in the twilight. It was too damn early to be up on a Monday morning, but she wasn't going to chance even not being stunning, in case Tyson Morgan paid her a visit.

Her heart rattled in her chest and she closed her eyes. Her mind drifted to yesterday morning when she was under him, their bodies pressed together. That wouldn't be a horrible way to start today either, she thought as she swung her legs over the edge of the bed and stood up.

Of course, if he didn't appear on her doorstep maybe he'd drop by her store. That might be even better. She was always on her game when she was at work.

Pearl turned on the bathroom light and started her shower. Today was going to be stellar.

Monday mornings were good for business. Lucky girls who were proposed to on Friday or Saturday night flooded Pearl's store on Monday mornings. There weren't very many sales, but there were connections made with these overly excited women. They would all be back over the next few months, and they'd bring their excited girlfriends, who would also get married some day. They would rent their tuxedos for their grooms and their groomsmen. Of course, the mothers of the bride and groom would also need dresses. Meeting new brides was one of her favorite things in business.

During her early afternoon lull, Pearl sat in her back room, at the small table, having a sandwich from the deli down the street. On the table, she had her planning notebook, the one she was recording all new store plans in.

She'd have twice the room at her new location. There would be room to do multiple fittings if she hired another person. They could carry twice as many dresses and even have the tuxes in store. There was so much to think about.

But then her mind wandered to her new business partner.

Would he come around more? Would he bring business to them—somehow?

Pearl pressed her fingers to her lips. It was hard not to think about it when her morning had been filled with hopeful women who were in love. She'd never been one of them—hopeful. Men came and went in her life. She shook her head. Why would Tyson Morgan be any different? They'd only passed through each other's lives, really she had nothing to build these fantasies on, but she couldn't help herself.

Tyson Morgan wasn't the kind of man she usually dated. Those men wore suits and drove fancy cars. They were clean shaven and well spoken. So what was it with this man who drove an old farm truck, wore worn out work boots, and a beat up baseball cap that turned her head? He'd consumed her every thought since he'd walked into her store on Friday. How much more could she take of this?

When the bell above the front door chimed, Pearl's heart rate shot up. She'd waited all day for him to appear—was this it?

She fixed her lipstick in the mirror and walked out to the main room to find Lydia standing there with a bottle of champagne in her hand and two glasses.

"We close tomorrow!"

Pearl smiled. "Tomorrow?"

She nodded. "My brother gave us enough to secure the mortgage on the building and do a lot of renovations."

"He'll be meeting us there then?"

Lydia set the glasses on the counter and began to unwrap the cork. "No, it's just our names on the title. The paperwork is being drawn up now by the lawyers for us all to sign regarding his investment."

"Oh, well that's fine then."

Lydia pulled the cork from the bottle with a pop! They both laughed as she poured them each a glass.

She picked up the glasses and handed one to Pearl. "Here's to partnership."

"To partnership." Pearl tipped her glass to Lydia's.

"We're going to make so much damn money," Lydia giggled as she sipped her champagne. "Already I have three women who have called me wondering when the reception hall will be ready."

"Three?"

Lydia nodded. "People already know what we're doing, and they can't wait. This is going to be big," she said sipping again. "Big."

Pearl liked the sound of that. She liked making money, and she loved her job. Hearing Lydia go on about the plans ahead of them seemed to ease Pearls anxious heart hoping that Tyson would walk through the door. Suddenly, she had plenty to think about. There was no room for the distraction of a man right now—even if he was her partner.

Chapter Twelve

Tuesday afternoon, Pearl met Lydia after work for celebration drinks and document signing. Wednesday, they met with the realtor and finalized everything before they signed the title to their new building on Thursday.

Friday, Pearl walked on air as she pushed through the front door of her shop. In two months she would be driving the other direction to work, and she'd be selling wedding dresses in her new store.

She could hardly remember a time when she'd been so giddy about anything.

She'd no more turned on the lights when the front door opened, and a flower delivery man walked through with the largest bouquet of roses Pearl had ever seen.

"I have a delivery for Miss Pearl Walker."

"That's me," she said walking toward him.

He handed her his clipboard and indicated the line she was to sign on. She did so and then took the enormous bouquet from him before he left.

Who on earth could have sent her these?

She set them on the counter and inhaled their beautiful smell as she searched for the card.

Congratulations on your new location, partner.

She checked the envelope for any sign of the sender. Certainly, it had to be from Lydia. It had been blatantly obvious that Tyson had no desire to come back around after they'd their very short interlude over the weekend.

She'd text Lydia and thank her for them. But before she could retrieve her cell phone from her purse, the store phone began to ring, the UPS driver began carrying in boxes, a bridal party arrived to pick up their dresses, and their tuxes, and then Sunshine walked through the door.

"Good afternoon," Pearl smiled as she walked toward her and couldn't help but pull her in for a hug. "It's so nice to see you."

"Thank you." Sunshine returned the smile. "I wanted to bring this to you and thank you again for all you did for me this past weekend." She handed Pearl an envelope.

"It was my pleasure."

"It meant the world to me. You'll never know just how thankful I was for what you did."

"So, how was the wedding?"

Tears pooled in Sunshine's eyes, but the smile remained genuine on her lips. "It was better than I could ever have imagined. I don't think if I had planned the wedding for a year it would have been any nicer."

"That's wonderful."

Sunshine nodded to the envelope in Pearl's hand. "I had pictures printed for you so you could see the dress through all the generations. I may be biased, but I think for my wedding it was the most beautiful."

Pearl pulled the photos out of the envelope. The first picture was of Sunshine and her new husband. "You looked radiant."

"I did, didn't I?" she giggled.

The next picture was obviously her parents' wedding photo. "Your father was military?"

Sunshine nodded. "Wasn't he handsome in his uniform?"

"Very." She lifted her eyes to meet Sunshine's. "How is he?"

The color turned in Sunshine's cheeks, and the tears were back. "He's already in hospice. I don't think he will be with us much longer. He was very brave on Sunday. It shows in his eyes."

"A soldier until the very end."

"That's my father," she said proudly. "We're going to wait on a honeymoon and even a reception. Perhaps in the spring, I'll feel more like celebrating."

Pearl thought of telling her about the reception facility they would have by then, but thought she'd better wait. With remodeling, you never could be sure how long things would take to be finished.

She turned her attention back to the pictures. Just as Sunshine had promised, there were pictures of different brides at different times in the same dress. What a beautiful tradition they had passed down she thought. Pearl realized she'd never even seen her mother's wedding dress. She wondered what her mother had ever done with it.

The final photo was Sunshine and her entire family.

Pearl studied the photo closer. "Phillip Smythe is related to you?" she asked noticing the man on the outer edge of the photo.

"You know my uncle?"

Chills traveled down Pearl's back. "Officer Smythe is your uncle?"

Sunshine nodded with great enthusiasm. "Isn't he a great man?"

Pearl wasn't sure what she was supposed to say to that. In fact, she'd never met anyone with a worse disposition than that man. Rumors had always run wild when it came to Smythe and how he treated women. And there was simply something creepy about him. Perhaps it was the way he acted whenever Lydia was around. She knew Lydia's take on him. She despised the man. However, when Officer Douglas Brant kidnapped Pearl's sister Bethany, it was Officer Smythe that quickly realized what had happened, and she credited him with saving Bethany's life. Well—she had saved her own life, but things could have been much worse without Smythe. It was hard to hate him completely.

Knowing she couldn't gleefully respond to Sunshine's comment about her uncle, Pearl slid the photos back into the envelope and noticed the writing on the front.

"Calligraphy? Did you do this?" she asked examining the writing.

"Yes. My mother used to do it, and she taught me. I was going to do it for all of my invitations, but, well, we didn't send any out."

"Would you ever consider doing this? I mean people are always looking for someone to write up their invitations and address them. No one has this skill anymore. It's a lost art."

"It is?"

"Yes. You might give it some consideration. I could certainly pass your name around."

Sunshine bit down on her lip. "That would be kind of fun. And after this week, I sure could use something fun."

"Give me your phone number. When things settle down for you, we can talk. Besides, when I move my store, there will be a lot of new bridal businesses in the same building. You never know what might happen."

For the second time in a week, Pearl watched Sunshine walk out of her store with a smile. It only solidified that Pearl loved what she did. Not every bride's story was like Sunshine's, in fact, hers was completely rare. But Pearl knew she'd touched her life, and that meant something.

As she turned back to the counter, she was met with the beautiful blossoms that filled her store with such wonderful fragrance.

She'd gone for her phone earlier that morning to text Lydia, and here it was early afternoon, and it was the first time she'd had a chance.

Thank you for the roses. That was very thoughtful. Pearl xoxo

She set her phone on the counter and began filing the invoices that had accumulated on the counter when Lydia texted back.

What roses? I didn't send roses, but I did talk to the florist that is moving in. I'll tell you about it. Late lunch tomorrow after you're done at work?

Pearl's skin warmed. They hadn't been from Lydia. That meant only one other person could have sent them.

Lunch sounds nice.

Pearl scrolled through her phone and looked for Tyson's number, which she didn't have. She looked at the time. There were no more appointments for the day, and all of her deliveries had arrived. It was past four o'clock, and with that, she decided to take a drive out to the Morgan's and thank Tyson for the flowers.

Pearl had decided to drive directly out to the Morgan's. She'd never actually been there, but she knew where she was headed. If you took the first right off the long dirt road, you went to Tyson's house. If you kept going you'd end up at her grandfather's, well, now it was her uncle's she supposed. Oh, she'd heard her father's side of things. He was hell bent on them selling the house, but that wasn't fair, she thought. Her uncle had raised his family in that house, and he'd been the one to take care of her grandfather until he passed. Her father hadn't done anything but make everyone's lives miserable. Perhaps a few months ago she would have stood on her father's side, had he put up an actual fight. However, now she wasn't so sure. The other side of the Walker family deserved that house and the land they worked. They were a true family.

Pearl shook the thought away.

As she neared the Morgan's, she could see the enormous house come into view. Her breath caught. Lydia and Susan had talked about it over lunch a few times, but she could never have imagined it was that grand.

The dirt road gave to a paved driveway that circled in front of the enormous house. The front doors were the size of the entire front of her house. Her hands began to shake as she came to a stop behind Tyson's pickup truck. At least, she knew he was home.

Pearl put the car into park, unbuckled her seat belt at the same moment her door flew open. With a muffled scream, she looked up to see Tyson glaring down at her.

"What are you doing here?" Tyson snarled at her.

"I...well...I just..."

"Turn the engine back on. You're not parking here," he slammed the door.

Pearl blinked away the tears that had quickly come to the surface and burned her eyes. She turned the car back on and swiftly threw it into reverse as the passenger door opened.

"Whoa! Don't run me over," Tyson growled as he slid into the passenger seat and shut the door.

"What are you doing?"

"Drive up the road and around the house. There is another road that leads to the barn."

"If you're too busy, I can..."

"Drive," he barked.

Pearl backed away from his pickup and drove around it to the road he'd pointed out.

In silence, they drove, at least, another mile down the private road to the barn that stood as majestically out in the field as the house had.

"Park over by the door." He pointed to a small door that looked as though it might enter into an office.

She did as he'd demanded and then parked the car.

For a long silent moment, they both just sat there until she got up the nerve to say what she'd come for.

"Thank you for the flowers."

Tyson rubbed his hand across the back of his neck. "You're welcome." He let out a long ragged breath. "I'm sorry about that. My grandfather, well, he's…he's in a mood," he said.

"I'm sorry. I should have called. I mean I tried to, but, I should never have…"

He cut her words short as he came across the center console and planted his mouth on hers.

Her breath caught as Tyson cupped her face in his hands and drowned her nerves with a kiss that had heat crawling up her body.

"Don't be sorry. Don't ever be sorry," he said resting his forehead to hers. "C'mon. Come in with me."

He opened the door and slammed it again before walking toward the barn. He looked back at her, and she realized she hadn't moved. How could she? She was overwhelmed with a dozen emotions.

Eventually, she gathered her senses and climbed out of the car. Shutting her door, she followed him into the barn.

She had been right. The door led to a private office, which she thought was nicer than any office in any high rise she'd ever seen.

"Yours?" she asked.

"Yeah."

"It's nice. So this is where you come to work every day?" she pried as she looked around the room.

"It's where I hide mostly." He moved to her and wrapped his arms around her waist. It was equally as quick as the embrace had been in the car. Enough so that Pearl staggered back before she was able to rest her hands on his chest.

Tyson bent to kiss her gently on the lips. The moment both confused and soothed her.

"I've been thinking about you," he said softly, still holding her close.

"You have? I thought you were mad at me or too busy for me. Or just not interested," she said with her voice dipping into the emotion she was feeling. She locked eyes with him, and she saw his go sad. Taking a breath, she continued, "I haven't seen or heard from you all week. And the last time I saw you, well, let's just say I thought you were *very* interested."

He let a slow groan rattle from his throat as he closed his eyes for a moment and then reopened them. "Lydia thinks it's best if we don't see each other since we're partners."

Pearl grit her teeth. "That's sensible," she agreed and hated it.

"And I told her that's how it would be."

That ripped through her, and she ached. "Then why are you holding me?"

"Because you're here."

She swallowed hard. "Why did you kiss me?"

"Because I couldn't stand not to." He gently kissed her again as if to make a point.

"I just wanted to thank you for the flowers," she managed with a shaky voice. "It was very thoughtful of you."

"You're going to do great in the new location. It's a nice place."

Pearl pushed back so she could gather her thoughts. "You've been there?"

He nodded. "A few times. Lydia is very excited about it. I met the realtor and signed what I had to sign."

Pearl pinched the bridge of her nose. "So you only ignored me because of Lydia?"

"Yes."

"Then I shouldn't be here." Pearl pushed her shoulders back and tried to swallow the disappointment that was brewing in her belly. "She's probably right, you know. It would get very messy if we got involved."

Tyson nodded as he moved toward her. "You and I come from very deceptive families. They lie and cheat to get what they want."

Pearl willed away the threat of tears. She was Byron Walker's daughter. And Byron Walker's daughter didn't cry when things weren't going her way—or when someone pointed out reality.

"You're right. Our families do that. You and I, and Lydia," she added, "aren't like that. If she thinks this is a bad idea, then we forget about it. We go on and…forget about it." Her voice shook as Tyson moved in even closer now, scooping her up with her legs wrapped around him and pressed against the wall.

His mouth came back to hers in a fury of heat and need, and she responded in kind. As the heat rose in her belly, she fought off the voices that told her to push him away, but instead she wrapped her legs around him tighter.

His fingers gripped her hips, and his hard body pushed against hers.

This was wrong. They had both just established that this wasn't a good move. They were all going to get hurt. There was so much more at stake here, but she couldn't stop. There was a desperate need to keep him close and feel his body pressing against hers.

Tyson sucked in a hard breath and looked at her. "What she doesn't know won't hurt her," he said gasping before taking her mouth again with his.

Thank God that's how he felt because Pearl was sure she was going to burst.

Chapter Thirteen

When Tyson had watched her drive up the road, he'd had all intentions of turning her back down it.

As his hand skimmed the skin just under the hem of her shirt and her fingers worked up into his hair, he remembered the promise he'd made to his sister. Then he thought about how he was going to break it.

Was this what had driven his biological mother, Eric's mother, mad—passion? Had she given up her child over lust? Was that what he was doing?

The bonding of the Walkers and the Morgans was one thing when it came to nailing the son-of-a-bitches that had been messing with them. But hard feelings and family secrets had torn the families apart for years. Having sex with a Walker wasn't going to mend it.

Pearl's legs were tight around his waist. Her lips were on his neck and her skin soft under his fingertips. A moan escaped between them—from him.

It was so much more than burying a hatchet. He'd done that. The moment he accepted his biological mother's fate, Eric as his brother, and the lie his mother, father and grandfather had fed him his whole life had been the moment the feud between families didn't matter.

But Pearl was Byron Walker's daughter. That did make a huge difference in the house he was raised in.

However, as her fingers began to work the snaps on his shirt, just as they had a week ago, none of it mattered.

This was Pearl. She was a mystery wrapped in a beautiful package. She did things to him, physically, without ever having to touch him. She did things to him mentally that he just couldn't explain.

Susan had been on his case to get that damn tux fitted. He'd held off as long as he possibly could. Since finding out Pearl's cousin was his brother, he'd spent his share of time around her. A fire had begun to fuel months ago, and he didn't want to feel its burn.

It was stupid. He was lonely, he thought, but then retracted it as he moved his hand up under her shirt and cupped her breast.

The moan now came from Pearl.

This was crazy. This lust put them both into the same category as their families—liars.

He winced as she gently nipped at his skin and he absorbed the pleasure of the pain. There was no stopping the momentum of what they had started. And why should he?

They were grown adults, and they were about to make a very adult decision—one he couldn't wait much longer for.

He lowered Pearl to her feet, and her eyes met his. "You're not going to stop are you? You're not going to say we can't."

He brushed his hand over her cheek. "I don't want to."

"Then don't," she said as she pressed her mouth to his. "Where can we go?"

The years peeled away, and he felt seventeen again. Sneaking around and finding pleasure in the body of a willing and beautiful girl.

He took her hand and led her to the couch on the other side of the room. Oh, this had surely been his escape for years. The big screen TV that hung above the fireplace and the small kitchenette allowed him to stay in that space as long as he wanted. He couldn't help but wonder if his grandfather even knew about the setup he had. Though he oversaw everything in the family's business, he very rarely left the house.

Still, Tyson couldn't help but want to keep him out.

Pearl positioned herself on the couch as Tyson stood.

"Where are you going?"

He smiled back at her. "I'm not leaving. Just locking the door—in case."

She batted her eyes at him and licked her lips. "Okay, hurry."

He did as he said he'd do and locked the world out. For this moment, it would be only him and Pearl. For this moment, it would be shutting the world away and embracing the moment that they might later regret.

When he turned back toward her, she was lying on the couch, her blouse unbuttoned, and the *breath of life* tattoo moved as her breathing increased.

The closer he got to her, the more intense her blue eyes became. Her full lips parted as if she waited for him to seal them with his.

For a moment he merely looked down at her, wanting to capture this moment in his memory.

"You're stunning," he said, his eyes on hers and not on her body.

The corner of her mouth lifted into a seductive grin. "Now's your chance to see that tattoo on my back."

He'd released the bad girl, he realized. Now the question would be, would he be able to keep up with her?

~*~

The day had quickly gone into the night, or so it had seemed. Pearl lay entangled in blankets on the floor of the barn office, in front of the fireplace, which they'd turned on more for ambiance than heat.

Tyson's body was curled up behind her. He brushed her hair over her shoulder and placed a precise kiss on the base of her neck. That sent a chill straight down her spine.

"I don't know if I have enough energy to continue," she said with a breathy voice replaying the afternoon of making love in her mind. "But we could try."

He chuckled. "We haven't used the shower in the bathroom yet."

Now she laughed. "I think it's the only area we haven't hit yet."

His hand skimmed down her side and over her hip. "Chinese symbols on your rib cage. Angel wings low on your back. A rose on your ankle and an infinity symbol with a dangling heart on your thigh. Have I seen them all?"

Her stomach did a little flip thinking about him *seeing* all her tattoos. He'd done much more than that she thought, remembering the kisses he'd feathered over her skin, lingering at each tattoo.

"I think you've seen everything," she said rolling so that she could face him. "The scar down your back, the one on your elbow, and another on your shoulder. No tattoos?"

"More accident prone than anything."

She ran her finger down his chest. "I doubt that."

"Lydia gave me the one on my shoulder. I was pushing her on a tree swing and got in the way. It knocked me down on a rock."

Pearl pressed her lips to the scar. "Your elbow?"

"Football."

"Your back?"

His eyes narrowed, and the playfulness faded. "Nothing awesome."

Pearl locked her gaze onto his. "I stumbled on something."

She watched as he processed it and she wondered if he'd trust her with the information.

"Horsewhip."

She didn't remark right away, but she couldn't keep quiet. "Not an accident?"

Tyson's lips tightened. "What does it matter?"

"It doesn't," she pressed a kiss to his lips. "Where do we go from here? I mean, I let you see my tattoos."

A smile crept onto his lips. "Are you willing to let me see them again?"

"Tonight?"

He shrugged. "And tomorrow. Maybe even the next?"

There was a new pattern to her heart beat. It had ramped up to a remarkable pace, and that thrilled her as much as his *promise* had.

Lying there naked, her body wrapped around his, and running through her head was only one question. "What about Lydia?"

He shook his head. "This isn't the time I want to talk about my sister."

"Kind of a turn off?"

"Extremely."

"Do you have food in that kitchen?"

Tyson's face scrunched up. "Microwave popcorn?"

"That's not good for you."

"Wasn't thinking I was going to be entertaining."

Pearl rolled him back so that he was flat on the floor and poised her body atop of his. "I'll tell you what. Why don't we try that shower and then I'll make you dinner at my place?"

There were no more words or promises before he maneuvered her up and carried her away toward the shower.

Chapter Fourteen

It was nearing nine o'clock by the time Pearl parked in her driveway. A few moments later, Tyson parked his truck, the nice one, on the street in front of the house.

Was it wrong to like the look of him parked there?

As she climbed from her car, she thought it would be very obvious who was at her house if anyone she knew were to drive by. They needed to decide how they were going to handle this. Either they were going to have a secret relationship, which had its enticements, or they were going to have to let Lydia know that they'd deal with anything that came their way. They were grown adults having sex and involved in a business. She didn't want to think they were involved more than the sex. That would be presumptuous of her. And her father always said, "If you assume, you make an ass of you and me."

She winced. She hated that saying.

Tyson walked toward her as she gathered her bag from the back seat. "Is my truck okay there?"

Maybe they were in sync with their thinking.

"It'll be fine. As long as you don't mind anyone seeing it."

He nodded slowly, his face highlighted by the street light. "I'm going to risk that, tonight. I'm not quite done being with you yet."

Her heart did that little trip again, and she was finding she rather enjoyed it.

"Thanks again for the flowers," she said, closing the car door and walking toward him. "I never would have gone to see you otherwise."

"Thanks for measuring me for that tux," he joked. "I never would have stopped in otherwise. I would have just waited for my brother to invite me to another dinner."

She couldn't fight the smile that surfaced. "That's why you came to dinners with everyone?"

"I think that since you know the reasons behind all my scars, and since I've kissed all your tattoos, then you can know that. Yes, that's why I went."

She moved closer to him until their chests were pressed together. "I've had sex with you more than just tonight, you know?"

His brows rose, and his eyes widened. "You have?"

Slowly she nodded as she licked her lips. "I've been dreaming about you for months."

Tyson cleared his throat. "Oh, really?"

"I don't measure everyone the way I measured you," she said, running her fingers up his chest. "I couldn't help myself."

"I hate the city," he said, and she stepped back.

Where had that come from?

"Why?"

"Too many neighbors. At least out at my place, I could drop you right on the ground and take you. Now I have to hurry you inside. We might as well forget dinner. That's not happening tonight."

He took her hand and hurried her up the front steps and through the front door.

~*~

There were mornings when Pearl wished she had a staff. Someone to open and someone to close. And someone to work on Saturday mornings so she could sleep in the arms of the man she'd brought home.

She felt the smile form in her heart long before it formed on her lips.

Tyson snored softly behind her, his body pressed to hers. She didn't want to move. She didn't want to end this moment.

Her alarm brought the radio to life, and she slapped her hand over it quickly, but he stirred.

"What was that?" His voice was low and gruff.

"I have to go to work."

He let out a groan. "I suppose that means I do too."

"I'm having lunch with Lydia today," she mentioned as she sat up and pulled the sheet with her to cover herself.

Tyson scratched his head and then his unshaven cheeks. "You sure do know how to keep me from thinking about you in an intimate light."

She wanted to laugh, but now it was too serious. "I just thought I should tell you."

Leaning up on his elbow, he let his hand trace the outline of her thigh under the sheets. "Are you going to tell her about this?"

She shook her head. "No. Not yet. I don't even know what *this* is yet," she said, and he agreed with a nod. It was then she realized she'd hoped he'd have an answer for that. Obviously, he didn't.

"I'll get my things and head out." He sat up. "Maybe we can have dinner this week."

The disappointment dropped into her gut. Didn't they have all weekend? "Sure. I'd like that."

"Dane is coming in tonight, for Susan and Eric's wedding next weekend," he added as if she weren't fully aware of that. "Gerald thought we should take Eric out tonight."

The lump in her stomach eased a bit. Perhaps he did have a reason to skip right over, *I'll see you later tonight.*

"Bethany has plans for all the girls on Tuesday," she said. "It seems Susan was very particular about having a classy night out and nothing too risqué."

Tyson chuckled. "Are you keeping to that?"

She shrugged. "I know a guy who will show up if I call, dressed as a police officer."

His eyes grew dark, and she knew what he was thinking. *I know a guy* was never a good thing to say when you were in bed with another guy. Especially when you were talking about a stripper.

"Maybe someone dressed like a police officer isn't the best choice for those girls. That might set Bethany back in therapy, and she doesn't need that."

Now she felt little. He was right. Bethany had been assaulted by a police officer and Susan's fiancé nearly killed by him. "A nice quiet dinner does sound nice."

He smiled. "I suppose I could be here when you got back, and I could be that *guy you know*."

"You'd do a strip tease for us?"

"For you," he smiled finally, and it eased the pain of the disappointment.

"I'm not expecting anything from you," she said, feeling as though she needed to.

There was a flash in his eyes. "I'm not expecting anything either," he said. "Last night was nice. I suppose it'll be nice next time too."

Any heat from a night full of passion had indeed been extinguished.

"I'd better get ready."

"I'd better head home."

For a long moment, they just sat and stared at each other before Tyson finally turned and picked his pants up off the floor.

Their impromptu night was over.

~*~

Her mind certainly wasn't on business. Pearl thought her first bride was going to cry when she'd brought out the wrong dress for her to pick up.

Somehow she managed through the rest of the day, even though she made her share of absent-minded mistakes.

Lydia walked through the door at two, a large cup of coffee in each of her hands. "Thought you could use a pick me up before lunch."

Pearl had nearly forgotten. "Sorry. I have one more pickup and then…"

Lydia held up her hand. "Don't apologize to me. My businesses run themselves, and I can drop in when needed." She smiled widely, and Pearl knew Lydia was proud of her successes. "Now, when the freaking water heater goes out at midnight, that's when business ownership is a pain."

She took the cup Lydia offered her. For a moment, she wondered if she should tell her about her night with Tyson. Then she thought better of it.

She'd taken a breath to tell her about Sunshine as well. Quickly, she remembered who Sunshine's uncle was, and that wasn't going to go over very well with Lydia.

This was the problem with keeping secrets, she decided. Everything she wanted to tell someone was only going to hurt them.

"It looks like the contractor will be starting on the building next week," Lydia said as she picked up a bridal magazine and began flipping pages. "We should have occupancy clearance soon too."

"I suppose I should learn what all of that means if I'm going to own a building."

Lydia smiled. "I understand it, and so does Tyson. Our mother is quite versed in building code," she chuckled.

"Will he be there a lot?" Pearl asked, needing to know Lydia's thoughts on it.

"I can't see him coming to town that much. He's just an investor."

"That's good," she said and hoped she was convincing.

Luckily she saw her last bridal pickup heading for the door. That should detour the conversation away from Tyson for a bit.

Pearl put on her professional smile and went to work.

Chapter Fifteen

Pearl was quickly learning that Lydia did nearly everything with a purpose.

She'd waited for Pearl to finish with her appointments and close up shop. She'd suggested a small café about four blocks away. They had decided it would be nice to walk.

"My mother brought me here last week, and I talked to the pastry chef. She makes cupcakes. They're her signature item," she added. "I know bridal showers and baby showers usually have something cute like that."

Pearl smiled. "They do. It's become a new fad to have individual items for people."

"Anyway, I'm always adding to my database of people to network with. Our little bridal mecca is going to be the talk of all Georgia."

Lydia's business aspect was something Pearl admired. She thought herself quite a business woman, but to watch Lydia's eyes light up when she had an idea, it was mesmerizing.

They sat and had lunch. Business was the main topic until Officer Smythe walked through the door to pick up a take-out order.

Pearl watched as Lydia's eyes followed him from the door to the counter. The woman behind the counter giggled at something he said, then gave her hair a toss, which only made the red in Lydia's cheeks deepen. She wondered if he even had seen them sitting there.

He turned from the counter and stopped. She was sure that was when he'd noticed them.

She could see Lydia's jaw tighten as he started toward the table.

"Ladies," he said nodding toward them.

Lydia said nothing.

"Nice to see you, Officer Smythe. Picking up lunch?"

"Yeah. Working on a case. Can't stand fast food. Thought I'd rather have a nice meal if I'm stuck behind my desk."

He was talking to Pearl, but his eyes were on Lydia, who had diverted her attention from him.

Finally, he looked at Pearl. "How is Bethany?"

"She's doing well. They're planning their wedding for September. Kent has another book coming out soon, so he's been preoccupied with that."

"I'll have to pick it up when it's out. I do enjoy his books." He glanced back toward Lydia, who still kept her gaze lowered. "Well, you ladies have a nice day."

"You as well," Pearl said before the thought of Sunshine's wedding pictures popped into her mind. "Oh, by the way, how is your brother?"

His eyes clouded, and he cleared his throat. "He's holding on."

"I've been praying for him."

He batted his eyes as if those words meant something to him. "I'll let him know. He'd appreciate that." He gave her another nod and left the café.

Lydia slowly lifted her head. "I hate him."

"I know you do. I don't know why, but I know you do."

Lydia's lips tightened. "What's wrong with his brother?"

"Stage four lung cancer. He's in hospice."

Lydia covered her mouth with her hand, and Pearl was sure she could see the shimmer of tears. "How do you know all of this?"

"I met his niece. Who is his brother to you?"

"Just someone I know. That's very sad," she added, picking up her fork and taking a bite of her sandwich.

Pearl had enough drama in her own family. She wasn't sure she wanted to invite more in by asking about Smythe's family and what he had to do with Lydia.

She picked up her iced tea and sipped. Perhaps some things were better off not spoken about.

~*~

Tyson pulled up to Eric's promptly at seven, as instructed by Susan. He was sure Gerald was heading up the bachelor party, so why the call came from the fiancée, he had no idea.

Pickup trucks were lining the road to the house and parked on the side. It made him chuckle. You knew that was a sign of a good party. The scent of meat filled his nose as he opened the door. It looked as if he were in for a steak dinner. He couldn't complain about that.

Dane pulled up behind Tyson, as he climbed out of his truck. "Hey, nice to see ya," Tyson called out.

Dane scanned a look at him, which he was used to. These boys needed to get over that Morgan/Walker riff.

"Thanks," he said wearily.

"Just drive in?"

"Yeah. I got caught up with road construction in Kentucky. Cost me two hours of travel time."

"Gotta love that."

Dane looked around. "So what's all this? I thought us guys were getting together."

"That's what I thought. I guess we'll see."

They walked up to the house, which was already lit up and noisy. Dane reached for the door and pushed it open.

It shouldn't have surprised Tyson that the house was filled with just relatives, and each of them must have driven their own truck.

Susan was setting platters of food on the table, and Glenda was carrying around beer bottles and handing them to everyone. She smiled when she saw them walk through the door.

"C'mon in," she said handing them each a beer.

"Mom, what are you doing here?" Dane asked as he leaned in and kissed her on the cheek.

"Susan and I are just getting you boys set up. We'll be out of here shortly. By the way, I've missed you," she said with a wink before walking away.

Susan looked at them. "Glad you two are here. Eric is out back working the grill."

"You're letting him cook?" Tyson joked as he kissed Susan on the cheek.

"We've had a few lessons. I can trust him now."

"I'll go say hello."

Tyson headed through the house and out the back door. There were Eric and his father standing over the grill. The sight hit him.

Tyson's father had been gone for years. He'd never shared a beer with him. He'd never hovered over a steak on the grill either.

"Hey," Eric greeted him. "You made it."

"I thought bachelor parties were supposed to be wild bar nights."

Both Eric and his father laughed. "I'm not much for that scene. Besides, I think Susan thought if she catered the party and turned on a football game, we wouldn't think about leaving."

"Works for me," Tyson agreed as he took a long pull from his beer.

Everett Walker moved toward Tyson, leaning against the railing of the porch. "I hear you bought into your sister's newest real estate buy."

"So much for silent partnership," he joked.

"Not much is silent around these parts. She has a good head for business," he complimented.

"She does. So does my mother."

Everett nodded. "She does as well. Even Constance had a good head for business."

Tyson felt the air whoosh from his lungs as Eric yelped.

"Jesus, that hurts," he said pulling his hand to his mouth.

"Burn yourself?" his father asked.

"Yeah, but I'm all right."

Everett gave him a nod and left them alone on the porch, returning to the house through the back door.

Eric watched his father disappear. "He slid that in there nice and easy didn't he?"

Tyson lifted his bottle to his lips and drank down the amber liquid inside. He felt the bubbles hit his stomach as the alcohol rose to his head. "That was a little awkward."

"He doesn't talk about her that much."

"I think that was for my benefit," Tyson admitted, thinking about his birth mother, whom he'd never known.

"Sure," Eric nodded as he flipped a steak. "Do you suppose we will ever see each other and not have to remind ourselves, in the back of our heads, that we're brothers?"

Tyson chuckled. "It does feel more natural to want to punch you in the mouth."

Eric grinned. "You did that already."

"Still feels good."

They shared a laugh, and that felt nice. They had, in fact, beat the crap out of each other less than a year ago, and now they were celebrating marriages and businesses. Who would have ever thought?

"You all are okay that I bought into Pearl and Lydia's building, aren't you?"

"I don't see a problem," Eric said as he turned a steak over the flames.

"I didn't either until your dad brought it up. That's two Morgans to one Walker."

Eric leaned in over the grill. "And she's Byron's daughter. That's worse."

Tyson felt himself wince. He didn't want to think that there was a better Walker to be with. There was nothing about her that made him think she was anything like her father. How could she be?

There was no reason to talk about business or Pearl. They'd agreed not to say anything about what had happened between them.

Tyson ran his hand over the back of his neck, then wiped it down the leg of his jeans. "I guess they'll be putting in the wells soon, over on our land," he said, changing the subject from their biological mother and Pearl.

"That's going to net you a pretty penny."

"It's all my grandfather's. I don't want anything to do with that."

"You'll get the land, right? In the end, that is."

"It goes to Lydia and me, but still. It doesn't feel right. The Walkers aren't the only people my grandfather screwed over through the years. I can't even imagine what he stole along the way to get the land he has now."

Eric pulled the steaks from the grill. "You're not like him, you know. You're not vindictive."

He wasn't sure about that. A year ago he would have gladly run Eric off the road, had he known who he was.

"I see my sister and my mother run legitimate businesses. Nothing under the table or greasing the palms of anyone to get what they want. They just work for it."

"Sounds like my father and grandfather. I don't know where my uncle got his business sense from."

"I guess there is one in every family."

Eric closed the grill and picked up the platter of steaks. "I suppose there is."

Chapter Sixteen

They had steak, which was what every man in the room was most excited about. Oh, they'd demolished Susan's well planned out trays, but it was Eric's steaks that won their hearts.

The small, newly built house was full of Walker men, Tyson noted as he pulled another beer from the cooler. All four of Eric's brothers, his father, his cousins, Bethany's fiancé Kent, and even his uncle Byron—Pearl's father, he reminded himself.

He could see the resemblance in the eyes, he thought as he studied him from across the room. Tyson wasn't sure he'd ever seen her mother. But they'd both lived in the same town their whole lives, it was possible.

It was obvious, though, that Byron Walker was the outcast among his family. Though everyone was cordial, it was his sons that kept him occupied with conversation.

"How are the cattle out at your place?" A man's voice came from behind him.

He turned to see Officer Phillip Smythe behind him nursing a beer. He looked as uncomfortable as Tyson felt.

"They're doing well. It helps when no one is killing them off." He referenced Douglas Brant, the fellow officer that had been killing heads of cattle, poisoning their horses, and had set fire to Eric's house.

"I'm embarrassed that he was part of our department," Phillip said. "I'm glad everyone is okay."

Tyson nodded as he sipped from his bottle. He wasn't sure why his sister hated the man so much. He wasn't that bad. Sure, he had a bad rap with the women in town and two ex-wives that had made sure no one thought much of him, but Tyson didn't mind him.

"I heard you bought into that building your sister purchased."

Tyson chuckled. How did that stuff get around so fast?

"Yeah, she needed an investor."

"Looks like it'll be a big wedding center."

That had him smiling. "She's referring to it as a wedding mecca."

"Mecca?"

"Yup. Bridal shop. Caterer. Floral. Reception hall. Anything you need for your wedding."

Phillip's brows drew together. "I thought she had the Garden Room for receptions. She needs two halls?"

Tyson shrugged. "The Garden Room is technically my mother's. Lydia won't be outdone by anyone, including my mother."

"Doesn't surprise me." He sipped from his beer. "Can't believe Eric is finally getting married. I was sure all of us were washed up."

Tyson bit down on the inside of his cheek. Yeah, he'd felt that way until he'd wrapped his arms around Pearl for the first time. Now he wasn't so sure.

Phillip looked at him. "Who are you bringing to the wedding?"

"No plans on a date."

"Me either. I'd ask your sister, but she hates me."

That was a true statement. "She'll be there," he said. "Maybe you can get a dance in."

Phillip snorted a laugh. "I doubt it. Not sure I should even ask. No need for a physical brawl at a nice wedding."

True enough. The thought then crossed his mind. He'd want to dance with Pearl. If they were going to keep their little affair secret how was he going to do that without letting on? There was no way in hell he could hold her close and not have his emotions show.

He finished his beer. He was old enough not to have to worry about what people thought in regards to his love life, right? Why worry about it?

Then he looked over at Gerald and Ben, who were deep in conversation in the corner. He had caught Gerald's eye before he looked away. More than likely they were having a conversation about him and how he didn't belong entwined in the Walker family.

The thought stung, but he didn't blame them—not one bit.

He finished his beer. "I think I'm going to head out," he said to Phillip.

"Me too. Not sure I belong here much, but it was nice they included me."

Tyson ran his tongue over his teeth and thought for a moment. "You off duty?"

"Yup."

"Why don't we head out to my place at the barn. I have a fridge full of import. I'm feeling the need to tie one on."

Phillip chuckled with a nod. "I could go for that."

~*~

Pearl sipped her wine, her legs tucked up under her, as she turned the pages of the bridal catalog full of next season's dresses. Oh, the necklines and the beading, she gushed over the detail. The budget would allow her to buy fewer top of the line samples this year because of the move. But, the move, in the end, would be worth it. Next season, she'd have more room, and a bigger budget, to buy more dresses.

The knock at her door came as quite a surprise. However, the kicked up thumping of her heart when she realized that she hoped it was Tyson at the door was more of a surprise.

She unraveled herself from the couch, stood, and walked toward the mirror on the wall. Giving herself a quick primp, she decided it wasn't much hope, but then again, he'd seen her tousled and wet with sweat. The thought gave her warmth that spread throughout her body.

Pearl moved to the door and pulled it open swiftly. She could feel the smile that formed on her mouth. Equally, she could feel it fade when she saw Lydia standing on her front step.

"Lydia, I wasn't expecting to see you. Is everything okay?"

Lydia's grin was large. In one hand she held up a bottle of champagne and in the other a roll of paper fastened with a rubber band.

"I have the final drawings from the architect for the outside of the building for our approval, partner. And some bubbly to celebrate. Interested in looking at it?"

The smile was back. "I'd love to." She stepped back and let Lydia through. Still holding on to that small shred of hope that Tyson was there too, she looked out the door, but no one else was around.

Pearl closed the door and walked back to the living room where Lydia had knelt down in front of the coffee table and rolled out the plans.

Pearl knelt down next to her and looked at the plans spread out on her table. "This looks complex."

"It's beautiful," Lydia beamed. "Here's your storefront," she pointed to the cornerstone of the building. "You'll have the most windows. Lots of natural light."

The building was two stories, and the plan was, in time, to rent out the private offices on the second floor. Lydia explained the updates that would be made to the building.

There would be parking in the rear of the building, which would lead to the reception hall. On-street parking would accommodate the store fronts. She had already signed Gia Gallo to a lease for the smaller store two doors down from Pearl's store. Susan had signed a lease to use the kitchen that was attached to the reception hall. Next week Lydia would meet with the florist and discuss a possible lease.

"It's coming together." Lydia sat back on her heels. "Within six months, we will have everything brides need. They won't have to go anywhere else."

"I like it."

Lydia grinned. "So do I. How about that champagne?"

Pearl stood, picking up the bottle as she did. "I have some strawberries we could have with this."

"Oh, that sounds classy," Lydia said, following her into the kitchen.

Pearl pulled down two flutes from the cupboard and set them on the counter as Lydia began opening the bottle.

"I think Tyson is going to be impressed with the designs," Lydia reached for the kitchen towel and placed it over the top of the bottle before pulling the cork out. "I think we'll be able to buy him out within a year."

"Buy him out?" Pearl asked as she opened the refrigerator and pulled out the bowl of strawberries. "Is that the plan?"

"It is for me. He doesn't want to be part of this. He's got other things to think about. Besides, he's not an in town guy. I think it makes him crazy to drive out here."

Any exciting buzz that might have been zipping through her had fizzled. "Well, if that's the plan."

"Are you taking anyone to Susan and Eric's wedding?"

Pearl set the bowl of strawberries on the table and sat down as Lydia did the same. "I'll be too busy making sure all the dresses and tuxes fit just right. The last thing I need is a date."

Lydia plucked a strawberry from the bowl and bit into it. "I figure there will be a wealth of Walker men in tuxes to choose from. Which of your brothers should I ask to dance," she laughed.

Pearl lifted her glass. "You can't go wrong with any of them," she said believing wholeheartedly that the statement was true.

"That would be a hoot, wouldn't it? Me and one of your brothers?"

Lydia laughed, but Pearl drank down her glass of champagne. It was innocent banter, but did Lydia even hear what she was saying? Tyson had said she didn't want him seeing Pearl, but she was sure Lydia didn't know anything about them. And, her brothers weren't involved in their business. However, she ached to tell her that just that very morning, Tyson had awakened in her bed.

Lydia sipped from her glass. "I think Tyson should take a date. Maybe it would make him more comfortable. He's feeling a little out of sorts being thrown into the Walker clan."

"They don't judge him," Pearl defended.

"I know. It's just a lot to take in. We had a good upbringing. Our parents loved us and never did we think he wasn't their son."

"You don't have to be born to people to be their child."

"I think that's the only thing that keeps him calm about it. He was close to our dad. He took it hard when he died, but he promised to carry on in his footsteps, which is why he puts up with my grandfather. And my mom feels horrible for never telling him."

"They didn't see a reason to."

"But that might have been wrong too." Lydia sipped from her glass. "It makes you think, though. What else in your life isn't like you think it is?"

Pearl filled up her glass and took a strawberry. What would Lydia think if she told her about sleeping with her brother—their business partner?

Chapter Seventeen

Sunshine filled the bedroom by the time Pearl opened her eyes. Her head throbbed from the amount of champagne and wine she and Lydia had consumed the night before.

But it was time to celebrate. They had the keys and the plans to a fantastic building. Pearl's new store was going to be brilliant. She couldn't wait to go in and just stand in the space with her designer.

Lydia's enthusiasm was equally contagious. Pearl had only ever invested in her own business. But to know that she would own the building where others would thrive in their businesses too, that gave her a giddy little kick.

She wondered if Lydia was always this excited over business deals. Did she celebrate every adventure with champagne and was she still asleep on the couch?

Pearl managed to land her feet on the floor, pull on her robe, and stand. She stood there a moment gaining her balance before she started downstairs.

The smell of coffee filled the air, and she quietly thanked God that Lydia had the sense to make some.

She walked into the quiet kitchen, looked at the clock. It was one o'clock in the afternoon. How had that happened?

Pearl took down a mug, poured herself a cup of coffee, and walked into the living room.

The blanket Lydia had used was folded nicely with the pillow set atop of it. But instead of Lydia sitting on the couch watching a movie on her TV, there sat Tyson.

"Ah, you're awake," he winked at her as he turned off the TV with the remote.

"What are you doing here?"

"Lydia called and asked for a ride to my mom's. She said she was severely drunk and not able to drive."

"When did she call you?" Pearl winced at the volume of her own voice.

"About six o'clock this morning."

"And you came back here and let yourself in?"

He grinned. "Do you mind?"

"No," she replied softly. She sipped her coffee and let it steady her a bit more. "I told her she didn't have to go anywhere. She was welcome to stay all day. I had nothing going on."

Tyson stood and moved to her. "Damn you are sexy when you're hungover."

She growled. "I feel like crap."

"And I thought I drank a lot last night," he chuckled as he brushed a strand of hair away from her eyes.

"The bachelor party?"

"More like my pity party," he confessed as he ran his hand down her arm. "I didn't stay long at Eric's. Smythe and I headed back to my barn and did quite a job on my beer collection."

His hand slid down until it reached her hand and he interlaced their fingers. It was intimate, and it sent a tingle surging through her.

"Why were you having a pity party?" she asked.

"I just don't belong yet. They were cordial," he quickly added. "But..."

"You're a Morgan."

"I'm a Morgan," he confirmed. "In time, it'll be entirely normal."

"Not every Walker thinks you don't belong."

He locked eyes with her. "Any one of them in particular?"

Pearl swallowed hard. "I think you belong—with me."

Swiftly he moved in and wrapped his arms around her, pulling her closer as she held her coffee mug out to the side to keep it from spilling.

"That means a lot."

"I should brush my teeth," she said lowering her head.

"I don't mind. I could look at you all day, just as you are."

Pearl bit down on her lip. "Isn't it kind of risky for you to be here if Lydia is in town too?"

He winked. "Her car is here. I think we have some time."

She wrapped her free arm around his neck. "I could use a shower."

A smile spread wide on his lips. "I could use one too," he said as he pressed his mouth to hers.

~*~

A devious smile permeated his lips as he drove out to his mother's house for dinner. He'd managed to spend the entire day entangled in Pearl's arms, and it had been worth the minute chance of getting caught by his sister.

They'd showered, wandered into the bedroom, made their way to the couch, and into the kitchen. Clothes were certainly optional all day, and that had been only one bonus, he thought.

He needed just to tell Lydia he was seeing Pearl. What would it hurt really?

Then his conscience kicked in. She'd asked him not to. She'd made it a point to say she didn't like the idea, and he'd chosen his sister over Pearl—or so he'd told her.

Hell, he was no better than his parents at lying.

He could feel the heat rise on the back of his neck.

The flash of him sitting with his sister, telling her that she was his family, and he'd always choose her, stirred in his mind. He'd had no intentions of keeping that promise, so why had he made it?

The windows were open at his mother's house. She always did love fresh air. Even in the winter, she'd keep her windows open the littlest bit.

He parked his truck and climbed out as his mother opened the front door.

"I could get used to you coming to town more often. Driving out to your place wreaks havoc on my paint job."

"I think I'll be coming around more," he said hoping she didn't read anything into it. "I've thought maybe it's time for me to leave the house anyway."

"You're plenty old enough to make that decision. In fact, to put my two cents worth in, you should have moved out when you were twenty. Your grandfather has just been keeping you under thumb."

"Thanks, Mom. I know that."

"I'm just making conversation," she continued as he walked up the step and kissed her on the cheek. "You smell good. A little flowery, but..." She winked.

"Don't read into that," he warned as he walked into the house.

But the little hum that followed him let him know she wasn't going to let that down.

"Where is Lydia?"

"Oh, she's around. She slept in pretty late. Guess she had a good night."

"I think she and Pearl were celebrating."

Her mother's lips puckered. "Do you think her going into business with a Walker is a good thing?"

"Nothing wrong with it, Mom."

"I know, but there's bad blood there."

"Not anymore. Don't forget, I'm blood with a Walker too."

She huffed out a breath, which meant she didn't want to go down that road.

He walked to her kitchen and pulled a bottle of water from the refrigerator. "I think this Walker/Morgan thing is old news anyway. I'm a partner in her business too. I don't question it."

"I know. You've got a good business mind too."

That was a compliment he was proud of, especially coming from his mother, whom he considered one of the smartest business women he'd ever known.

Lydia walked through the kitchen in a pair of her mother's sweatpants and a Victoria's Secret PINK shirt. His mother was obsessed with the brand though he thought she was much too old for it.

Since Lydia wore her hair short, it didn't even look disheveled where she'd run her fingers through it so many times.

"Thanks for coming to get me," she said with a yawn.

"I'm sure Pearl wouldn't have minded you hanging out all day."

"I'm sure too, but Mom and I had some business to discuss." She exchanged glances with their mother.

"However, she slept through most of it."

Lydia shrugged. "It's a good year all around for me."

Tyson watched as both women smiled. This was how they communicated. He wished his father was still alive so he might have someone to keep secrets with as well. Of course, he wasn't sure he still would share the secret of Pearl.

"Are you going to tell me what's going on then?"

Lydia sat down in one of the kitchen chairs and rested her head in her hands. "I'm buying Mom out of the Garden Room," she said with a yawn.

He turned to his mother. "You haven't had that more than a year. Why are you selling it?" Then he turned to his sister. "And you needed me for your last business deal. How can you buy her out? And why are you?"

His mother's cheeks pinked. "Lydia doesn't think it's wise for me to get involved with my business partners."

"She's made that clear enough," he said, then wishing he hadn't. "I didn't realize you had a business partner. Other than Lydia."

That was when his mother rubbed her hands together, for show, and he noticed the new piece of jewelry dominating her left ring finger.

"What is that?" He pointed to her.

Her eyes opened wide, and she smiled wide. "Oh, look at that. A big beautiful ring." She looked down at it.

"Mom, what's going on? You certainly aren't getting married are you? And who is it? I didn't even know you were seeing anyone. Your track record after dad hasn't been stellar."

Lydia stood, took a moment to balance, and then took his bottle of water out of his hands and sipped from it. "You should get out more. She's been seeing Les for a year now. You haven't bothered to notice."

"I've had a few dramas in my life in the last year," he quipped.

His mother stomped her foot as she would when she was irritated. "Now you two stop it. We are all grown adults here. I have a nice man in my life, and he wants to marry me. I said yes."

It stung. He should have known she was seeing someone. He should have met him. He should have given his blessing.

Lydia had spun this so that it was his fault too. That didn't sit well either.

"I want to meet him," he demanded.

"You will. At dinner tonight."

"Tonight?"

His mother pursed her lips. "Did you have other plans? Maybe it has something to do with that floral smell on your clothes." When his mother wanted to fight nasty, she could. He'd always figured that was how she'd stayed sane living under the same roof as his grandfather, even after his father had died. It also gave her a great advantage in business.

Lydia moved in closer and sniffed his clothes. "I don't smell it."

If he let out a sigh of relief, he'd be caught. "That's because she doesn't know what she's talking about," he lied. "I'll be at dinner. Where and when?"

His mother lifted one brow, and that had meant she'd won this battle. Was there anything more uncomfortable than meeting a man who already wanted to marry his mother?

He caught Lydia's scrutinizing eye. Yes, he thought. Lying to his sister made him very uncomfortable.

Chapter Eighteen

Having spent the afternoon with Tyson had been an amazing treat, but now Pearl was hurrying to get ready and look presentable. She hadn't planned on a day wrapped in his arms, drowning in his kisses, ignited by his touch. She'd planned on working on her new location, which included dinner plans.

She'd been in this position one too many times, she thought as she checked herself in the mirror. A man comes along and suddenly focus on what was important got lost.

This new location was going to be twice the size with twice the inventory. It was going to take a lot more to make a living, not to mention that she was now partially responsible for the entire building. There wasn't going to be anyone to call when the roof leaked or toilet backed up. It would be on her head now, and of course, Lydia and Tyson's too.

But regardless, she'd be one of the people making the phone calls to get things fixed, and she'd be one of the people paying for the repairs.

The very thought had her stopping to take a long, deep breath. Why did she nearly hyperventilate every time she thought about it?

When the doorbell rang, Pearl looked at her watch. The man was prompt, as always.

She hurried to the door and pulled it open. Standing on the front step was Donald Jefferson looking very handsome and put together in what she could only assume was a custom suit.

"I could set my watch by your promptness," she said taking his hand and pulling him through the front door.

"Time is money."

"You've always said. So why do you set up dinner dates?"

"One has to eat, right?" His held his hands up in gesture then gave her a wink.

His blond hair had more product in it than hers did. His eyebrows were more groomed. His attire was classier than the restaurant he'd chosen, but she knew for a fact the man had a crush on the maître d', and that was why he'd suggested it.

"I have some great drawings for you to look at," he beamed. "So let's go so I can show you my designs."

"I have a budget."

He let out a deflated breath. "Your mother would never tell me that."

"My mother would somehow steal money from my trust fund to pay you."

"She does have good taste," he chuckled as he opened the front door.

All Pearl could do was shake her head. Yes, her mother's taste in everything had always been exquisite.

As Pearl closed the door and locked it, she noticed that Lydia's car was gone. A small pain shot through her chest. Tyson had to have dropped her off, yet neither of them stopped to say hello—or goodbye.

It wasn't worth getting upset about. She knew how things were. It had only been a week of involvement with Tyson. She couldn't expect him to check in with her all the time. And again, there came the disappointment with getting involved.

~*~

Tyson pulled up in front of the restaurant cursing the fact that he'd even agreed to show up.

His mother should have told him she was seeing someone. There were responsibilities when you had children. It didn't matter if she was nearly seventy years old. She should have told him.

Tyson parked his truck and sat in its quiet for a moment. He couldn't blame his mother. Tyson had been a real ass with his attitude about heading into town for years. There were sometimes weeks, maybe even months, when he hadn't even driven to town. He was more comfortable wallowing in his solidarity in his barn.

Then there was the fact that he too had his own secret.

An open mind was needed when he walked into that restaurant. His mother deserved her happiness. And he deserved his.

It might be just the right opportunity to mention that he was seeing Pearl. In fact, he'd been interested in Pearl for a long time, so maybe it was a little more in depth than *interest*.

Just because his mother didn't mix business and personal feelings didn't mean he couldn't. It wasn't as if he was going to spend all day in their *wedding mecca*. In fact, he didn't even care if he ever got his money back for the investment. He'd have given the money to Lydia no matter what.

He climbed out of his truck, and his step was light as he walked toward the restaurant.

As he walked inside, he noticed Lydia right away. She waved him toward the table where she sat with their mother, and a man whom he could only assume was Les, the man his mother was going to marry.

The last time he was nervous was the morning he walked into Pearl's store. The butterflies that were attacking his stomach were nearly equal to the moment Pearl ran her hand over his body while measuring him for the tux.

The man stood as he approached. That was a good sign, he thought.

Tyson walked directly to his mother and kissed her on the cheek.

"Oh, you're right on time. I'm glad you joined us," she said as if he were given a choice.

Tyson kissed her on the cheek. "Of course, I'm here."

His mother reached for his hand and gave it a squeeze. "Tyson, this is Les Watson, my fiancé."

The man next to her held his hand out to Tyson. "It's a pleasure to meet you. I have heard a lot about you," Les offered.

Tyson shook his hand. "Nice to meet you." He certainly couldn't offer the same pleasantries as he'd only heard of the man earlier that morning.

As he released Les's hand, he pulled out the chair situated between his mother and his sister. Before he took his seat, he gave his sister a gentle squeeze on the shoulder.

Tyson ordered a beer and a steak then sat back and listened to wedding banter. It seemed to be a theme in his life right now.

A half hour later, he'd decided that he enjoyed the man his mother had chosen. He wasn't sure if that was the man himself, or the look in his mother's eyes when she looked at him.

"I think I'll stop into that little bridal shop of Pearl Walker's," his mother said as she sipped her wine. "Lydia speaks highly of her."

His sister grinned. "She's the best at what she does," she said. "Mom doesn't want anything traditional. Pearl has an excellent selection non-traditional. Just classy."

Tyson only nodded.

His mother patted his hand. "I'm going to ask Susan, Eric's fiancé, to cater at the wedding."

"I can't see that you'll be disappointed," he said.

"I know, this must bore you," she smiled at him.

"Are you buying my dinner?"

"Of course."

"Then I can be humored," he joked, and she laughed. That made him happy. His mother deserved to smile and laugh.

~*~

Donald was an expert at many things and picking out fine wine, and excellent restaurants were one of them. He'd asked for a booth with good lighting and in a corner so they could work. Pearl was fairly sure he just wanted to scope out the restaurant, but all she cared about was the plans he'd drawn up for the store.

He set his drawings in the middle of the table.

"You will have so much light," he said as he raised his hands in the air. You'll have two *banks* of windows. Not just one big one. Natural light is going to be an amazing addition to what you can offer."

"It looks like there is one less dressing room."

"There is. Personal touch, sweetheart. Do you need four dressing rooms? Work with three and then it won't seem so crowded. I like what you have in your store now. The little sitting area. Grow on that, honey."

She liked it. "What is this corner?" she asked as she pointed to the area he'd put a crown on and added glitter.

The smile on his face could have lit the room when she'd asked. Donald scooted out of his seat and around to her side. He draped his arm over her shoulders and put his head against hers. "Darling, that's the tiara corner."

"Tiara corner?"

"Okay, the veil section, but, honey, you need more tiaras. Every girl wants one."

The man was an adorable genius, she thought as she pressed her hands to his cheeks and kissed him quickly on the lips.

Donald flipped the page of his sketchbook and pointed out his design for each dressing room.

"Pearl, what are you doing here? I never saw you walk in."

Pearl looked up and saw Lydia standing at the table.

"We're going over the drawings for my new store. This is Donald Jefferson, my interior decorator."

Lydia held out her hand to shake his. "Nice to meet you. Lydia Morgan. Pearl's business partner."

"The building is magnificent," Donald beamed. "Sit. You have to see what I've done."

Lydia smiled and took the seat where Donald had originally occupied.

Pearl took a moment to look around. "Who were you here with?"

"My mom and her fiancé."

"Your mom is getting married?"

Lydia nodded. "Tyson had never met Les. So it was time."

Pearl felt the blood drain from her head. "Tyson was here with you?"

"Yeah. He just left." She shook her head. "He's such an ass sometimes. He's more like my grandfather than I think he'd like to admit. One minute we're having a nice meal and then once the check was paid, he all but bolted out of here."

Pearl clenched her hands under the table. Had he seen them and he didn't stop? She grit her teeth. She hated drama in relationships—if that's what it was. Why didn't he talk to her? Then she looked at Lydia, who was listening to Donald speak of the store.

They had to tell her. They couldn't go on like this anymore. It wasn't fair to any of them. Really, would Lydia make that big of a deal about it?

She sat back in the booth. Maybe right now wasn't the time. It would be better to be established in her store before she got into her first big fight with her partner.

However, she did need to talk to Tyson. If he did see her, why didn't he stop and say hello?

Chapter Nineteen

The moment Tyson hit the county road, his foot pressed down on the gas.

What in the hell had he thought was going on?

One minute he's having a meal with his family and the next he's watching the woman he'd just slept with kissing some other man.

He wasn't going to have it. That was that. Pearl Walker had a reputation and damn it if he didn't walk right into his own heartbreak.

He slammed the heel of his hand against the steering wheel. What had he been thinking? He knew what she was like. He knew her reputation.

She was all business on the outside, but she was a Walker—Byron Walker's daughter. That alone should have had him running from day one. No, he took her out for drinks. He let her feel him up while she measured him. He kept showing up at her doorstep.

Tyson knew he was the idiot. He'd gotten to that age where he shouldn't even give a crap about wanting someone in his life. Damn it, he was there. He'd been there for years.

Women were just trouble. And now, here he was, thinking more about a woman than he should have. He'd gotten involved, and it pissed him off that he'd even thought there was more to it than there was.

He'd had moments in the past week where he missed her. It had ached—he'd missed her so much when he wasn't with her.

Hadn't he even told his mother, he'd been thinking of moving to town? That was all because of Pearl.

She'd brought out things in him he thought were long dead. Feelings had been resurrected—and now stomped on.

When he had her wrapped in his arms, and she gently smoothed her fingertips over his skin, there had been a moment where he thought he could have stayed there the rest of his life. He hadn't wanted to leave. He'd have married her at that moment if he'd thought to ask.

Tyson's truck tossed him in his seat as he flew over the first cattle grid. It was then he reminded himself to slow the hell down. What good was it going to do to kill himself on a dirt road? No woman was worth that.

It shouldn't be a big deal. So, he had a fling with his brother's cousin—his sister's business partner—his business partner. It happened.

They were both adults. No need to get all bent over what he'd seen or what she'd done.

They'd had a few hot times. They'd had a few sweet times too.

Sure they'd cross paths for the rest of their lives, but who didn't have at least one awkward moment during family events?

His foot lifted from the gas pedal more, and his breathing began to calm. Maybe it was time to think about taking a date to Eric's wedding.

The house was dark, as usual, when Tyson pulled up to it. He'd grown up in that house, but it certainly didn't feel like home. He wasn't sure it ever had.

He rubbed his eyes and ran his hand over his unshaven chin.

Tonight he'd begin to make changes, he thought. He'd worked to have the perfect setup in the barn, and that might as well be his home from now on.

He drove past the big house and out to the barn wondering if his grandfather would even notice that he hadn't returned to the house. How many days would it take him?

The barn was dark too, but it didn't seem cold as he pulled up in front of it.

Tyson parked his truck and climbed out. Walking toward the door, he pushed it open. That felt like home.

He flicked on the light switch and suddenly he swore he could smell her. He winced. Of course, he could. They'd been intimate in nearly every corner of the room. It should be a good memory, and he was going to store it in his brain as such. There wasn't any reason to dwell on it.

Throwing his keys on the table, he kicked off his boots and then fell onto the couch. Pulling his cell phone from his pocket, he turned it off. No need to be disturbed for the rest of the night. He didn't want to think again until the sun came up the next morning.

~*~

Donald loved to talk. He was full of ideas for everything, and he'd engaged Lydia in a deep conversation about the building.

They had sat at the restaurant for nearly three hours discussing new plans. He had a few ideas for the garden room as well.

But somewhere, mid-presentation, Pearl just wanted to go home.

Checking her phone every five minutes wasn't helping her anxiety either. She wanted to talk to Tyson, but it was nearly ten o'clock, and he hadn't called or texted. Maybe he just went home.

As they were wrapping it up, she excused herself to the bathroom and texted him. If she didn't have to be at work in the morning and didn't have a fitting at nine o'clock, she'd drive out to his place.

That too, was a bad idea. Lydia would certainly know what was going on if she followed her all the way out of town.

She'd just wait for his call.

~*~

The morning had attached itself to the night before. Pearl hadn't slept at all, and as she passed in front of the trifold mirror, she realized it showed.

She smiled at the mother of the bride that sat on the small sofa drinking a cup of coffee. Her professionalism wasn't about to be displaced by the bags under her eyes.

When the bride came out of the dressing room, Pearl saw the tears well up in the mother's eyes.

"Oh, honey, you look beautiful," the mother cried.

"I like this one, Mom. It's like yours. Look." The woman in the dress showed her mother an intricate piece of lace embedded in the dress and that had sent the woman into a full cry.

Pearl gracefully picked up the box of tissues and handed them to her.

"Thank you. Oh, to see your daughter get married…" she dabbed at her eyes. "This must be old hat to you, to see such beautiful women each day."

Pearl smiled. "It's what I love about my job."

And she did, but every once in awhile a mother, much like the one to her side, got under her skin.

It wasn't that the woman was now a babbling mess, it was that hers wouldn't be. Oh, her mother would have opinions on what she should look like, sure, but she wouldn't be emotional in the least.

Pearl batted back tears that began to sting her own eyes as the woman moved to her daughter and stood with her, looking in the mirror.

For the first time in her life, Pearl wished for that happiness. She wanted it. She craved it.

It would be different. She knew that. Her mother would make the day all about her. Her father, if he bothered to show up, wouldn't even be her first choice to walk her down the aisle.

Oh, she'd want a dress and a formal setting, but she had come to the conclusion, she only wanted to share it with the man she would marry.

Discretely, she excused herself to the front of the store and pulled her cell phone from her purse. There was still no call or text from Tyson.

Something had happened. Why wasn't he responding to her?

Chapter Twenty

Pearl was dressed and ready for Susan's bachelorette party. They had agreed to a tea party, and her sisters had both called and made sure she hadn't hired a stripper.

It bothered her that they'd think she would. Of course, ten years ago, maybe she would have. But she'd grown up. So why did everyone have to think she was going to cause trouble?

The Garden Room was set up for high tea, and the twinkling white lights on each of the trees illuminated the outdoor venue. She wondered, in the end, what the reception room at their new location would look like. Lydia certainly had a way of making it warm and unique.

Pearl stopped just short of the room and took it in. There was Susan, and unmistakably Susan's mother and her sister. Her sister looked just like Susan, only with blonde hair. Pearl had heard that Susan's parents were hippies, but she'd have to admit, she thought that meant 'were'. Her mother's hair was bright silver, straight, and hung to her waist. The dress she wore was bright in color and perhaps handmade. Each finger adorned a ring, and her arm clamored with bangle bracelets. But what Pearl noticed most, was the sparkle in her eyes. Susan's mother adored her, and she was genuinely happy for her daughter. It came through louder than any words ever could.

"Aren't you going in?" Her mother's voice came from behind her.

Pearl turned to see her mother standing beside her. Her hair was perfect, and so was her makeup. The suit dress was pristine, and the jewelry she'd chosen accentuated it perfectly.

"You look beautiful," Pearl complimented.

"Thank you, darling. Who is that in the sandals?" Her mother's voice dipped.

"Susan's mother."

Her mother hummed, but Pearl understood it. It was a displeased hum. Leave it to her mother to be judgmental on someone's looks.

Lydia saw them lingering in the corner and moved to them. She pulled Pearl into a warm hug.

"I loved meeting Donald," she told her. "He came by the building today, and we drew up plans for the reception hall. You're going to love them."

She knew she would. "He's very talented."

"C'mon. Let's get this party going."

Because Lydia and Bethany had been in charge of the tea, it was exquisite. The selection of drinks was just right, and the tea sandwiches were incredible.

"Susan," her mother began somewhere into her second glass of champagne, "you didn't cater your own bachelorette party, did you?"

Susan laughed and shook her head. "I had nothing to do with it. Bethany, Lydia, and Glenda did it all. They even made the sandwiches."

Bethany giggled. "I give all the credit for the food to Glenda. She's truly the master of the tea party."

Lydia raised her tea cup. "I'll second that. You are a genius when it comes to this sort of thing."

Glenda blushed. "I love to entertain. Thank you for letting me."

Pearl watched Lydia's face as Glenda spoke about teas and pastries. The woman was wild with ideas and they lit up her face when she had them. Pearl didn't have to ask her what was on her mind, she could read it. She thought Glenda's tea parties would be the perfect fit in their *wedding mecca.*

Pearl looked around the room at the women who had come together to celebrate Susan. Only Susan's mother and her sister were there from her side of the family. The rest of the guests were people Susan had met in Georgia or were related to Eric.

They certainly had a big family and an eclectic one at that.

Pearl's mother sat next to her brothers' mother and shared gossip. They'd been best friends before they became the wives of Bryon Walker. Somewhere after they'd become ex's they became best friends again and had stayed that way. Glenda, Eric's stepmother, was the perfect mother, in Pearl's opinion. She doted on her sons, and on Susan.

Lydia and her mother were very social. Each of them made their rounds from table to table to speak to each guest. Of course, there were Pearl's sisters, Bethany, and Audrey, but they sat at separate tables.

Audrey was cordial to Bethany, but she had yet to warm up to her completely. Though Pearl understood it, she didn't condone it. Bethany had moved to Georgia to be with her family—with them. She deserved to be included as much as possible.

Pearl figured Audrey was just jealous. Pearl had a great deal to do with the other women in the family. In fact, even Lydia's mother had already mentioned that she would be stopping in to look at wedding dresses.

It was at that moment when Lydia's mother mentioned her wedding, when Pearl froze. Usually, there'd have been no hesitation in setting her up an appointment, but she had realized that this woman was Tyson's mother too. Sure, not by blood, but she'd adopted him—raised him.

She talked to Pearl as a woman in need to a professional. There wasn't the slightest hint that Pearl was something more to this woman's son.

Pearl had another glass of champagne as she listened to the friendly banter going on around her.

She quickly realized the rest of the week was going to be all about getting Susan and Eric to the altar.

The wedding was on Saturday, so she would have to close her shop. That had taken some arranging too. It had crossed her mind to ask Sunshine to come in and just be present. But appointments worked out in her favor.

Wednesday, everyone would pick up their dresses and tuxes. The bonus there was, she'd get to see Tyson. Maybe he'd feel different about her "adjusting" the tux than he had about her measuring him.

Thursday afternoon there was a small spa day planned for the bridesmaids. Manicures and pedicures with the coordinating polish color. Audrey had arranged it at the salon she worked at.

Friday was rehearsal dinner at Susan and Eric's house.

Then, bright and early Saturday morning, she had an appointment to have her sister do her hair.

Just thinking of it all was exhausting. Seriously, she thought as she finished off the current glass of champagne, if she was ever to get married, she was just going to elope. She knew weddings and brides were her business, but there was just too much to think about. Grateful as she was that people went through it on a daily basis, she didn't want anything to do with it for herself.

Wednesday morning Eric was waiting outside her store before she had even made it to the door.

"Are you that anxious to get married," she joked as she walked toward him. "You want your tux first thing in the morning?"

He chuckled. "When you rise with the sun, you sometimes forget how early nine o'clock is to other people.

I've been in town an hour already. Ran into Smythe at the coffee shop and had a cup of coffee with him. His brother died last night," his voice trailed off.

Pearl's heart jolted in her chest. "That's horrible."

"He said he'd been in hospice."

Pearl nodded. "Smythe's niece told me. They had their wedding early so that he could be there."

"That's sweet. What role did you have in that?"

She shrugged as she unlocked the door and opened it. "I just had some compassion, that's all. She needed a dress altered, and I made sure that happened."

"You've always had a sweet side," he said as they walked in, but she didn't turn to acknowledge that.

Her soft side had been shadowed by her need to make her parents suffer through her adolescence and teenage years. But it was nice to know that someone understood her.

"Are you collecting all the tuxes?"

"Mine, Gerald's, Ben's, Russell's, and my dad's." He numbered off with his fingers. "Dane will be by later, and so will Tyson."

Just hearing that he was coming to see her lit a fire deep in her belly.

She walked toward the back of the store with him in tow. "It's unusual for there to be more groomsmen than there are bridesmaids."

"I think it's all crazy to tell you the truth, but this is what Susan wanted. I just wanted all my brothers to be part of it."

She turned to look him in the eye. "I think it's wonderful that you included Tyson."

"I spent my life hating him for no reason. The hate and secrets have to stop, and it starts with us. He's my brother. He should be in my wedding."

Pearl turned toward the rack of tuxes quickly. She didn't want him to see that that had brought her to the brink of tears. He was right. The secrets had to stop.

She gathered the tuxes for the men whom Eric had listed and then turned to hand them to him. "I'll be there to adjust if needed. Sewing kit in hand."

He studied her. "You live for this, don't you?"

"I love to see happy people."

"How big will your wedding be? A Royal affair?"

She chuckled. "I thought of that last night. If I ever get married, I'm running away."

He laughed. "I kinda think that's fitting for you. Do it all your way."

She nodded. That would be precisely the point.

It was going to be an evening of paperwork, Pearl noted, as the door to her store was never closed for long. Lydia had bounced in and out three times, once with Donald. A photographer Pearl worked closely with dropped by to check out the colors for one of the weddings she was shooting. And Gia Gallow had stopped in to introduce herself.

"I am looking forward to being part of the new location. Your sister Bethany was in my store yesterday, in fact. She was picking up a wedding gift for this weekend. She has been a regular customer," she said, her Italian accent dripping with exotic.

"The next few months can't go fast enough," Pearl laughed. "So where are you from originally?"

"Lucca. I grew up inside Lucca, so my family is steeped in tradition." Gia's smile radiated though Pearl wasn't sure what growing up *inside Lucca* meant. But she figured she'd have plenty of time to get to know her.

The door opened again, and Dane walked through. "Ah, another tuxedo pickup," she cheered.

He merely smiled with a raise of his eyebrows. "Most uncomfortable suit ever."

Gia turned and looked him over. "I guess you are the groom?"

Dane shook his head adamantly. "That would be my big brother. Can't say I'm anywhere ready to be the groom."

"I will bet the tuxedo will look wonderful on you. You have a handsome face."

At that moment, the handsome face changed into one of complete surprise. His eyes went wide, and his mouth dropped open before he spoke.

"Thank you." He held out his hand. "Dane Walker. I don't think I've met you."

The feisty Italian beauty jaunted her hand in his direction and took his. "Gia Gallow. I own *Treasures from Italy* around the corner. I will be in the new building with Pearl when it is ready."

Dane didn't say anything else, he merely held Gia's hand and stared at her until she pulled back and gave her long black hair a toss over her shoulder. "It was nice to meet you both. I will stop in again soon. *Ciao!*" She gave them a small wave as she walked out of the store.

"Close your mouth, Dane. She's gone now."

"This is what I get for moving to Ohio. I leave town and that," he pointed to her, "moves in. Just my luck."

As the day moved toward its end, she was well aware that she hadn't seen Tyson. He had two hours to pick up his tuxedo before she closed. Was it worth a call to Susan to let her know he hadn't come by?

No. That was childish.

She picked up her phone and texted Tyson.

I have your tuxedo ready for pick up. When will you be by?

She set her phone down and moved to her computer to put in her new orders.

By five, he hadn't texted, called, or shown up. Seriously? What was this man's problem?

This time, she was going to call him. As she picked up her phone and scrolled through her contacts, the door opened and in walked Tyson, full of attitude.

"I'm here. Where's the tux?"

She set her phone down and crossed her arms in front of her. "You're just going to bust in here and act like that? Where's my hello? Where's my *I'm sorry I haven't responded to any of your texts?*"

"Can I just get the tux?"

It had fallen apart, and she hadn't wanted to believe that. He'd given her a few good nights, and days, and that was all he could offer.

Pearl walked to the back of the store and retrieved the tux. "Do you want to try it on?"

"Pretty sure you got every measurement the first time. Can't see that it isn't going to fit."

She nodded. "I'm done for the day. Would you like to…"

"I have stuff to do. I can't be spending my time in town."

And that was it. She had been dumped and hard.

"I guess I'll see you tomorrow then."

"Looks like it." With that, he hung the hanger over his finger, flung the tux over his shoulder, and walked out of the store.

It would be childish to cry like a baby, but it was coming. She was going to burst like a broken pipe.

Quickly she locked the door, turned off the lights, and ran to the back room. Pulling a bottle of water from the refrigerator, she let the first tears fall. Soon there was a waterfall of them.

She sat down at the table and opened the water. She'd thought there was going to be something more between them. She'd become very rusty when it came to relationships, which was sad. Her business was all about making sure everyone else's day was perfect. She'd forgotten how to have perfect for herself. So what had made her think that Tyson was her perfect?

Chapter Twenty-One

It hurt more than Tyson could have imagined. He'd waited until the very last moment to go in and see Pearl. It should have been a warm feeling that crept over him, but it was ice that had squeezed at his heart.

He should have told her he wasn't someone to be played. If she was going to have a relationship with him, then it was supposed to be only him. But he knew her ways, so why had he gotten involved?

He took his time on the drive back home. What was there to hurry for?

His grandfather had, in fact, noted that he'd moved out to the barn. He was his crotchety old self when he'd read Tyson the riot act over it. Seriously, if he didn't make a living on the property, he'd just pack up and leave. As it was, his grandfather gave his opinion. Tyson had given his. Now he lived in the barn permanently. Right where his grandfather said he belonged—with the horses and their crap.

Lydia's truck and another car were parked outside the barn when he pulled up. Certainly she hadn't brought her horse home. Maybe she was as unhappy with the Walkers as he seemed to be .

That wasn't fair, he thought as he turned off his truck. He was only unhappy with one of the Walkers. No need to start a feud over one woman—again.

Either way, he wasn't in the mood for company. Not even his sister's.

Lydia's laughter filled the room as Tyson opened the door.

"Oh, good. You're finally back. I have to head to town for pedicures. Did you get your tux?"

"It's in the truck." It was then the man with Lydia turned so he could see him. It was the same man Pearl had been kissing in the restaurant. What in the hell were they doing?

"Come here. I want you to meet Donald."

Was it PC to kick the crap out of a man who was a guest in your house, he wondered.

"Hey," he gave him a curt nod and his sister obviously noticed, by the way her eyes lit in irritation toward him.

"Tyson, Donald is an interior designer. He's working with Pearl on the design of her store, and now he's working with me on the reception hall. I wanted to show you the drawings."

"I'm kinda tired. Why don't I…"

"No, no, no." Donald waved his hands in the air. "You must see what I've done." He slapped his hand to his chest. "You'll make me cry if you don't look."

Tyson stopped in his tracks. Had the man just batted his eyes at him and winked? Oh, dear Lord! Had he been throwing a hissy fit over some man who was more interested in him than he was in Pearl?

Hesitantly, he walked toward the table where they had pages spread out. There, in vivid color, was *Pearl's Bridal Boutique*.

"Has she seen these?" He looked up, and both of them nodded. "They're nice."

Donald stomped a tempered foot. "Nice? They are brilliant."

"Brilliant. Yes," Tyson agreed in a hushed voice. "When did you meet with Pearl to discuss these?" It had to be asked.

"I took her to dinner the other night. That was when I met our Lydia." Donald put his arm around her. "She's delish too."

Tyson cringed. Not at the gay man standing in his kitchen, but at his lack of trust when it came to Pearl. He'd completely written her off because she'd kissed this man. He'd dismissed her without asking questions.

God, he was a moron.

Donald cocked his hip and placed his hand on it. "Our Pearl hinted that she'd been seeing someone. She refused details, and I love juicy details." He winked at him again. "You're not our hot man are you?"

He took a breath to protest, but Lydia let out a hard laugh. "He is not seeing Pearl. Pearl is much too much woman for him."

"Hey," he responded in equal childlikeness. "No woman is too much for me."

But his sister's eyes remained light. "He promised me he wouldn't see her. We're all business partners, and pleasure doesn't mix with business. And I'm much more important than any cute woman. So he wouldn't dare go behind my back."

Donald gave a high hum. "I wonder who he is then."

"I'll have to find out. She didn't tell me she was seeing anyone," Lydia chirped with equal enthusiasm. "This is all news to me."

Tyson walked past them and to the refrigerator for a beer. Shit was about to hit the fan, and Tyson wondered how he was going to get as far away from it as possible.

~*~

The Haven was quiet on Thursday night as the members of Susan's bridal party filtered in. There were only three pedicure chairs and two nail stations, so they were dividing their times.

Susan waited for Pearl by the door and greeted her with a glass of wine. "Your sister was beginning to wonder where you were. I assured her you were on your way."

"I was ordering some flowers for a funeral."

Susan rested her hand on Pearl's arm. "Who passed?"

"Officer Smythe's brother."

"I didn't know. I'll make sure to send a card."

She imagined that Susan would probably deliver a meal to the family's home as well.

"It's about time," Audrey walked toward her. "You're ten minutes late."

"I'm sorry. But I'm here."

Her sister huffed out a breath and waved her toward the pedicure throne where Rachelle waited for her.

She climbed into the seat of the pedicure throne as Lydia rested her hand on her arm. "Everything alright?"

"Yeah, just had a stressful day. This will be a nice treat."

"I heard Phillip Smythe's brother passed away."

It was the first time she'd heard Lydia call him by his name, and without the hateful tone in her voice. "I heard that too. I sent flowers to the family."

"I should do that too. What else happened in your day?"

She wasn't about to tell her that her brother pissed her off, but that would certainly make her feel better. "It was just a busy day."

"I met with Donald, and we came up with some brilliant plans for the reception hall. He showed me what he'd been working on with your store too."

"He's very talented."

Lydia sipped from her wine glass. "Donald also said you'd hinted to having some man on the side." She raised her brows and grinned over her drink.

Pearl stared at her. "Why would he say that? I didn't tell him that."

"He seems to know something. So what are you hiding?"

Susan stopped as she was passing by and her eyes grew wide. "You're dating someone?"

"No. I didn't say that," Pearl argued. "Seriously, where is everyone getting their information?"

Glenda, who was in the third chair, groaned. "Rumors aren't kind things to pass around girls," she said as if they were twelve. "If Pearl has a man in her life that's her business, not ours. Though," she said lifting her wine glass, "if she wants to talk it through, she should."

Every one of them burst into laughter, except for Pearl. She most certainly didn't want to discuss it, especially now that he'd turned into some huge ass. But Glenda's mocking of the situation seemed to have defused the tension and suddenly they were talking to Susan's mother about essential oils, and Pearl's love life was forgotten.

Chapter Twenty-Two

The Walker house was designed to entertain. Tomorrow it would play host to a grand wedding and tonight to a rehearsal.

Pearl stood in the garden and looked at how it had been transformed into a beautiful sanctuary for Eric and Susan. They deserved to have such an elegant setting.

"It's beautiful, isn't it?" Tyson's voice came from behind her, but she didn't turn around. She was afraid to. He was just going to be a jerk, especially since they were going to be surrounded by his family.

"It's lovely," she said still facing the altar.

She heard his footsteps. A moment later she could feel his closeness.

"I owe you an apology."

She swallowed hard and pushed down the tears that threatened. "You do."

He took her hand and turned her to face him, but it took her a moment before she raised her head and looked him in the eye. ⋮

Tyson let go of her hand and tucked his hands into his front pockets. "I was a jerk to you yesterday. I had no right to be like that."

"Thank you. I don't know what happened, but it hurt."

"It was designed to." He rocked toward her, but she knew he was keeping his hands in a safe place. "I was hurt, and I didn't know how to deal with it."

"You could be more cordial. Besides, what did I do that made you so angry?"

Tyson took a deep breath. "You kissed Donald."

"I did?"

His eyes opened wide. "You most certainly did. I saw you do it. You cupped his face in your hands and kissed him right on the lips."

"When?"

Now his hands flew from his pockets and into the air. "At the restaurant the other night. I was there. I saw you kiss him."

She began to laugh. "I'm sorry. I didn't remember kissing him, but yes. I did that."

"Yes, you did."

"Donald is gay."

"I know," his voice had raised, just as hers had. "I know," he said softer.

"Why didn't you say hello?"

"Because when I saw you it ripped through me. I couldn't stand it."

She licked her lips and took the slightest step forward to close the gap between them. "You were jealous."

"Why wouldn't I be? You're seeing me."

The smile was automatic. She couldn't have fought it off. "I am?"

He rocked back on his heels again as if to distance himself. "Are you playing games with me?"

"No. I just want to make sure that you mean it."

"Would I have said it otherwise?"

"No." She wanted to reach up and touch him. She wanted to plant a kiss on his lips and cup his face, but she fought the urge. "We're okay?"

"I want to be," he offered. "I really like you. I mean really like."

Now she chuckled and held her hands to her chest where her heart fluttered uncontrollably. "I really like you too. And I mean *really*."

"Whatever happens this weekend, just forgive me for it now," he offered as he took a step back from her as if to provide space.

"As long as on Sunday we can have a long talk. I know how Lydia feels about us."

"She's very adamant about it," he said. "I don't see it being a problem, but she is my sister."

"Family means a lot. I understand that too," Pearl said, clenching her fists at her side, so she didn't accidently touch him.

They'd managed a few feet between them, and no one seemed to notice as Susan, her sister, her mother, and Glenda walked into the garden. Just then, Dane, Gerald, Ben and Russell entered the garden from the gate behind the garage.

There was laughter and talking. Staging and restaging. By the time Lydia walked outside, Pearl and Tyson were nowhere near each other.

But she couldn't take her eyes off of him.

He liked her.

He *really* liked her.

Susan and Eric's house was packed with family—and only family after the wedding rehearsal. Somehow Pearl had found herself in the corner with Dane as they drank beer and ate Susan's food on sturdy paper plates.

"I'm sure she would have rather had a sit-down meal for her rehearsal dinner," Dane said as he looked around the crowded room. "Glenda didn't want her to have to clean the night before her wedding."

"Susan wouldn't have it any other way." She leaned in closer to him. "Her dad is quiet, but her mom is very social."

"She gave me a salve for my dry hands. It fixed them in one day."

They both laughed. "It's nice to have us all together. I've missed us doing this."

Dane nodded. "You're right. I think when grandpa was sick and dying we had a different focus. I wasn't sure the family was going to survive what happened with your father." He winced. "That was insensitive. I'm sorry."

"No need. Trust me. There is some embarrassment associated with it and not from him—from me."

"You've never done wrong. I don't think anyone associates you and him. I mean, no one thinks you're like him." He puckered his lips. "All of this sounds bad."

"I get it. All of his kids get it. We always wanted to be from your family. Aunt Glenda is the perfect mother and Uncle Everett is an upstanding man. My father is just lost." She shrugged. "I guess that's the best way to say it."

"It's good we all have each other. And you have your sisters and your brothers."

Pearl looked around the room. "I do. I'm very lucky. I'm just glad Bethany has us too. I should count my blessings. I could have been left in this world to suffer alone, just as she had."

"See. Everything turns out for the best."

She changed the conversation from herself to Dane, asking him about living in Ohio. He stared ranting about the job he hated and the horrible apartment, but she wasn't sure she heard a word.

Tyson stood across the room in the other corner with Lydia, who was talking a million words a minute, no doubt explaining the new *wedding mecca* to Susan's sister. Pearl couldn't hear it, but she could see her hands in the air and the smile on her face, probably talking business. However, she was sure that Tyson had no idea what she was saying. His eyes were fixed on Pearl and hers were fixed on him.

This was going to be the longest weekend of her life, she thought with a smile.

Chapter Twenty-Three

Tyson was used to his family dynamics. His grandfather would dictate his expectations and the family would oblige. Of course, when Tyson thought family it meant his sister, his mother, and his grandfather. There had never been extended cousins, and now he knew why. But having a house full of relatives was beyond him—and he liked it.

The rehearsal dinner had started nearly three hours ago and yet no one had left. They were still talking, drinking, and eating.

He would have thought Susan would have kicked them out hours ago. Didn't a bride need her beauty sleep? Obviously, it wasn't a worry.

He finished his beer and walked to the kitchen to throw the bottle in the recycle bin. Perhaps it was fate that Pearl was the only other person in the kitchen.

"Quite a party huh?" She was grinning at him, and it warmed him.

"Yeah. I was thinking I should head home, though. I still have to get up and tend to business before getting all dolled up in that monkey suit."

She laughed quietly. "I'm looking forward to seeing you in it."

Tyson wanted to go to her and just wrap his arms around her. It was killing him to keep his distance.

Dane walked in taking the last pull of his beer. "Mom said to recycle this."

Tyson pointed in the direction of the bin.

Dane dropped the bottle in with the others and gave a big exaggerated stretch. "I'm toast. I'm heading home."

"I was thinking about doing the same," Tyson admitted. "I'll walk out with you."

Dane moved to Pearl and gave her a hug. "See ya in the morning, cuz."

She laughed and planted a noisy kiss on his cheek. "It's nice to have you home."

"I sure do miss it," he said as he headed out of the kitchen.

Tyson stood staring at her for another moment, but he didn't dare cross the room toward her. "I'm heading back to my place—the barn," he said. "I'll see you later." He gave her a wink and thought if she could read between heavily clouded lines, she'd catch his drift. If not, then it would become a literal term.

Pearl watched Tyson walk out of the room and heard him say his goodbyes. Did she dare interpret what he'd said as he'd be waiting for her? What if that wasn't what he'd meant at all?

She took a deep breath and decided that it didn't matter. They'd exchanged *really likes*. They had argued about jealousy and petty things. That cemented a relationship, didn't it?

But as her cousins left, and her sisters departed, she found that only she and Susan's mother were left to pick up after the party when Eric finally excused himself to check on the horses.

"You don't have to help me with this. I can get it later," Susan argued.

"Later is your wedding day and you can't be worrying about this," her mother told her.

"I don't mind staying," Pearl added. "I have nothing else to tend to." She hoped she was convincing because it was killing her not just to run to Tyson's place.

With the three of them, the job at hand only took a half hour. Soon she was kissing Susan goodbye and Susan's mother was giving her a long, spiritual hug.

She headed out onto the dark road in the opposite direction from town—headed toward Tyson.

~*~

It had been more than an hour since Tyson had left the party. It seemed as though Pearl hadn't gotten his message. Who would have blamed her? He'd been an ass to her, apologized, then tried to secretly tell her to stop by without using any such words.

He decided he'd better get to sleep. That wedding was at noon, which meant he had to be at the house by ten so they could take all sorts of pictures. There was still a lot of work to be done before he even showered and shaved the next morning. Eric might appreciate if his wedding pictures didn't have his groomsmen with bloodshot eyes.

Tyson turned off his TV and unfolded his sleeper couch. Maybe a Murphy bed would be a better choice in time. Especially now that this was his primary residence.

Just as he'd arranged the pillows the way he liked them and pulled off his shirt, he heard the sound of tires on the road headed toward the barn.

He walked to the window and watched as the headlights grew closer.

His body began to pulse. Nothing would be more disappointing right now than if his sister was pulling up to his place.

But as the car came closer and parked next to his, relief washed over him. She'd understood his cryptic message, and she'd come to him.

Tyson opened the front door and leaned against the doorjamb as she parked her car and climbed from it. Even in the dark, he knew the outline of her body and in his mind could see her face clearly.

As she came into view, she smiled. "Was this what you meant by *later*?"

"You have no idea how much I hoped you'd figure that out."

She sauntered toward him. "I'm not sure I should stay, though. It's been made very clear I shouldn't have been spending those intimate moments with you."

"You're right. She certainly has an opinion. But so do I," he said, moving to her and swiftly pulling her into his arms. His mouth took hers as her hands went directly to his hair. He could feel her heart beat against his chest. No part of this wasn't consensual. Lydia was going to have to deal with it. Tyson was going to take Pearl—and he wanted to keep her too.

As it did every time the man touched her, Pearl's head swam with his kisses. No man, ever, had made her feel the way he did when he was around her.

He pulled her through the door, closed it, and then pressed her up against it. His body was warm, and his weight against her lit up her core.

"This is your last chance to go home. If you stay, you're not going to get much sleep," he said nipping at her neck.

"I knew that driving over here," she said breathlessly as he lifted the hem of her blouse and touched her skin. The very contact made her knees go weak.

Tyson lifted the blouse up over her head and discarded it to the floor. "I meant it when I said I *really* like you," he grinned, but his eyes were dark.

"I meant it too. And now I think we both know what it really means."

"Yeah," he said hoisting her up to his hips as she wrapped her legs around him and her arms around his neck.

"We'll get to that. I'm not going to worry about you kissing other men now. I think we got that sorted out."

"Indeed."

"And we'll worry about my sister later," he promised as he carried her to the fold out bed. "For tonight, it's only you and me. We can talk future tomorrow."

He laid her down beneath him and took her mouth with his again.

She wanted to read more into his promise of a future, but for tonight, she'd just let him make love to her over and over. After all, she *really* liked him.

~*~

Tyson's breath was heavy on her neck as her alarm on her cell phone chimed. She reached for it and turned it off as he pulled her closer to him.

"Why is it when you sleep in my arms that damn phone wakes us up?"

She eased against him. "Because you and I are very busy people. But this time, it's because I have to get to town and begin getting ready for a wedding. You do too."

He groaned, then pressed his lips to the base of her neck. "Have to attend to the animals first. I guess I never was meant for sleeping in."

She rolled in his arms to face him. "Sleep at my house tonight. Tomorrow I'll help you with the animals."

He opened one eye and squinted at her. "City girl coming to the ranch?"

"If it means spending time with you."

"It's a deal."

"Good." She kissed him quickly on the lips then rolled from the bed.

She gathered her clothes and dressed as Tyson watched her. Desire had her fighting off the urge to climb back in that bed with him.

"I'll see you later in that well-fitted tux," she said as she leaned in to kiss him goodbye.

"I may need to rethink that re-measurement opportunity."

She nudged his nose with hers. "I'll see you at the altar," she joked, but his eyes only grew darker. "I'm just kidding."

"Maybe give that some thought," he said, but she didn't respond. What did that mean? "Go. You'll be late for your hair appointment, and your sister will be furious."

She could only nod now as she pulled back and walked out of the barn.

The sun was rising, making a grand appearance on the horizon. It seemed fitting after a warm night.

Pearl climbed into her car, started the engine, and drove away with his words playing in his head. *Maybe give that some thought.*

Chapter Twenty-Four

Tyson had rolled from the bed and made it to the bathroom. He brushed his teeth as if the cows and horses would care about his morning breath. He slipped on a pair of jeans and went to retrieve the shirt he'd worn the night before.

As he folded up the bed and pushed it back into the frame of the couch, he heard tires on gravel, a door close, and footsteps. The door opened, and he joked as he folded the blankets, "I thought we were in a hurry. I don't think I have time for another…" he stopped as his sister walked through the door.

Her eyes were red and filled with tears. That much he could see in the dim light.

"Lydia, what's wrong?" He moved to her, but she threw her hands up as if to stop him with some force.

"You are a damn liar! Promises to me mean nothing!"

He took a breath to ask her what she was going on about, but he stopped. Suddenly he knew why she was mad. "Lydia…"

"Don't Lydia me. You promised me you wouldn't act on your feelings for Pearl. You said you'd choose family. You said you'd choose me."

"I know what I said."

"And it meant nothing to you. My businesses are very important to me. You can't just go around sleeping with my business partners especially when I asked you not to."

Tyson scrubbed his hands over his face. "This is ridiculous. Let's sit down and have some coffee and…"

"Are you kidding me? I'm not going to sit down and discuss this with you. I asked for one simple thing."

"It wasn't simple."

"It should have been." She turned and pulled open the door.

Tyson moved quickly and pulled her back in. "We're grownups. We can discuss this as such."

She yanked her arm from his hand. "Buy me out."

"I didn't want to buy in, remember?"

"You had all intentions of being with her the whole time, didn't you?" She studied him. "You have been with her the whole time."

"This doesn't have to be a problem."

The tears were back in her eyes, and they hurt more than her yelling at him. "You're no better than Grandpa or our parents are you? Keeping secrets is a way of life for you. It's no wonder none of you can be happy. You don't understand what it means to be true to your word about anything."

Then she turned, walked out of the barn, and slammed the door behind her. He let her go.

He'd been so wrapped up in himself all, this time, he never realized that the secrets his parents and his grandfather had kept had hurt her too.

Lydia was an honest person. All she'd asked for was honesty. He'd owed that to her from the beginning.

He heard her truck speed away. He shouldn't have broken his promise after he'd made it. But when he said he really liked Pearl, he'd meant it. Maybe the words should have been different, but they were the ones he could use.

But Lydia—Lydia was all he had. She'd never failed him, and all he'd done was fail her.

Tyson searched for a shirt. He had work to do and then his brother's wedding. This couldn't have come at a worse time, he thought. They all respected Susan and Eric too much to ruin their wedding with their problems.

~*~

Making sure she early for her appointment, Pearl walked through the door of *The Haven*, checked in with the receptionist, and then poured herself a cup of coffee from the complimentary coffee station.

She looked at the shelves of fancy shampoos and nail polishes. Pearl was a sucker for a new nail lacquer. Just as she'd chosen a color she liked best, her sister appeared.

"I'm ready for you. I have Lydia right after you. Clare is doing her makeup. Joyce is working on Bethany right now."

"Wonderful." Pearl set down the bottle of polish she'd been admiring and followed her sister back to her station. As they passed Bethany she gave her a little wave. Oh, what she'd give to have beautiful, red hair like Bethany. Then it made her wonder. "What are you going to do with Lydia's hair? It's short."

"We worked on curling it and putting some cute clips in it to match the rest of us."

"Very creative," she said as she sat down. "I'm lucky to get my hair to look good just to go to work. You do have a way of making people look fabulous.

Audrey smiled at her in the mirror. "Thank you. That means a lot."

The last few times she'd been around her sister Audrey had been snippy. Perhaps there was a story there. She'd like to ask, but why ruin a perfectly good morning?

After all, she'd awakened in the arms of the man she loved and—she stopped thinking about it and gripped her hands tightly together under the cape her sister had just flung around her.

She most certainly wasn't going there in her head. Love was a big commitment for her and for Tyson. They liked each other. That's what they'd said. *Really liked* each other.

"Are you okay? You just went white. Can I get you some water?" Her sister asked, placing her hands on Pearl's shoulders.

"No. Sorry. Guess I had something on my mind."

"Okay. Don't freak me out like that. Remember when I had that old lady die in my chair in cosmetology school? I don't take it lightly when someone loses their color in my chair."

Pearl forced a smile on her face and let her sister get to work with her masterpiece.

Forty-five minutes later, Audrey had made Pearl look like a princess. Curls were pinned in just the right places. Accents such as a small sprig of baby's breath and a daisy adorned the masterpiece.

"All I need is a tiara," she said admiring herself in the mirror.

Bethany joined them. Her beautiful red locks had been styled just as Pearl's had.

"I think I might cry," Bethany said.

"Well do it now," Audrey offered. "Clare is waiting to do your makeup, and that will certainly be too late."

Bethany and Pearl walked to the other room where Clare was finishing up Lydia's makeup.

"Oh, you look beautiful," Pearl sighed as she looked at Lydia, but the compliment hadn't brought any joy to Lydia's face.

Clare finished the last of Lydia's makeup. "All done. I think Audrey is ready for you."

Lydia waited for Clare to remove the small cape from around her neck, then walked past both Pearl and Bethany without a word.

Bethany watched her walk away. "What's wrong with her?"

"I don't know. Should we talk to her?" Pearl watched her disappear as she sat down in Clare's chair.

Clare put the small cape around Pearl's neck. "I asked her if she was okay, and she says she has a mess to clean up. That's all she said. Doesn't seem as though she's too much for talking about it."

Pearl nodded as Clare gathered her makeup tools.

She understood just wanting to handle things in her life. But she couldn't help but wonder what had gotten into her like that. Well, they were business partners. She would certainly talk to her when the moment was right.

By the time Clare had finished her makeup, Lydia had left the salon. She guessed that there hadn't been too much to do to her hair.

Audrey had told Pearl that Lydia was just quiet today and that she shouldn't read anything into it. She supposed she was right. They might be business partners, but she didn't know Lydia all that well. She'd butt out until Lydia was ready to talk.

~*~

Why did women always have to run in bunches and why were they always late, Tyson wondered as he looked at his watch. He looked like an idiot standing outside the Walker's house pacing in his tuxedo and shiny shoes. Susan had sent Glenda to make sure he was okay. Eric had happened by, dressed to the nines and looking mighty sharp as Tyson had told him.

Everyone from the bridal party had arrived except Audrey and Pearl.

Lydia had walked right past him and said not one word. He needed to intercept Pearl before it got out of hand.

He could see the dust kicked up from the road before he could hear the car. They'd both arrived in Audrey's car.

Tyson watched as she parked and then held his breath as Pearl climbed out in her bridesmaid'sdress and her hair all done up.

She saw him immediately, and her brilliant smile took over.

"I did get you the right size," she joked as she walked near him casually.

"Wow, Morgan, you do clean up," Audrey added as she walked past them and into the house.

He scanned another look over her. "You look beautiful. Though I'm not sure that's a good enough word."

"I think it does the job." She looked around. "What are you doing out here? I didn't expect any alone time today," she said with a wink.

"We have a problem." He swallowed hard. "Lydia knows about us."

Pearl's shoulders dropped. "That's why she's not speaking to me."

"You've seen her?"

"Seen her, yes. Talked to her, no. She ignored all of us this morning and..."

"Do you know what it's like to feel as though you were stabbed in the back?" Lydia's voice came from the doorway.

Pearl and Tyson looked toward her.

Pearl took a step in her direction. "Lydia, you have to understand."

"I do understand," she said curtly, stopping Pearl from advancing. "You both think so little of me that you'd go behind my back and sleep together. We're partners." She said looking directly at Pearl and then at Tyson. "And you're my brother. I should have been able to trust your word. But it means nothing to you."

"Lydia, you know that's not true."

"Do I?" She narrowed her eyes on Pearl. "I want to be bought out. I can't have you as a partner, so I want out."

Pearl's eyes widened. "I can't do that. I don't have that kind of money."

"Your lover does," Lydia snapped.

Tyson stepped up to his sister. "We are going to stop this right now, and we will talk about it tomorrow. This is Eric and Susan's day."

"Fine." She turned around and started for the house. "I assume that you'll get married behind my back too? It would be fitting."

"You're getting married?" This time, it was Susan's voice that came from behind them as she, her sister, and the photographer walked from the garden. Her eyes fixed on them and went wide. "You two? What did I miss? You're getting married?"

Pearl shook her head. "Misunderstanding. That's all."

Susan moved closer to them, leaving her sister and photographer behind. "I don't think so," she said smiling. "How long has this been going on?"

"Nothing is going on," Pearl said shifting a glance to Tyson.

Susan glanced his way as well. "Nah, something is going on."

Chapter Twenty-Five

The photographer had whisked Susan and Pearl away. Tyson stood alone again in the driveway contemplating what had just happened.

He didn't like this side of his sister. He'd rarely seen it, so he didn't quite know what to do with it either.

Tomorrow, they would all sit down and discuss what was going on. He wasn't about to cause a family rift between him and his sister over some woman.

That hurt to think of her in that way. She wasn't just some woman.

The door opened again and this time, Eric walked out to him. "You doing okay?"

"Yeah. Just have a lot on my mind. But it's not my day, it's yours." He made sure there was a smile on his lips. "You ready for this?"

"I am. Never thought I'd say it, but I am." Eric gave him a slight nod. "Are you?"

"For you to be married? Sure, why not?"

"I mean you."

Tyson fought off the urge to stick his hands in his pockets, as Glenda had been very strict about that ruining the crispness of the tux. "What do you mean?"

"I hear you and Pearl are getting married. I didn't even know you guys were seeing each other." He leaned in. "She's not pregnant is she?"

Tyson raked his fingers through his hair and sucked in a breath. "This is worse than high school."

"She is?"

"No." At least, he didn't think so. "No. And no, we're not getting married."

"Susan's sister was telling her mother that you were. And Bethany overheard and became very excited about it. Looks like you're getting married." He laughed and a moment later eased back. "But regardless of rumors, which I'll put a stop to…"

"I'd appreciate that," Tyson interrupted.

"You and Pearl?"

Tyson winced. It was out there now, and he saw no reason to deny it any longer. "Yeah. Me and Pearl."

"That's crazy. How long has that been going on?"

"Couple weeks. It's hit or miss. Lydia disapproves."

"Why? They're partners."

"That's the problem. Mom's track record of getting involved with business partners hasn't been a good thing."

"And now she's marrying her banker?"

Tyson nodded. "Yeah, but she sold off her businesses so that she didn't lose anything."

Eric rubbed his hand over the back of his neck. "I fall in love, decide to marry a woman, and suddenly I'm totally out of the loop," he laughed. "I think Lydia is a smart woman. She'll accept it."

Tyson shrugged. "She holds grudges. She hasn't said a decent word to Phillip Smythe in fifteen years."

"I'm out of the loop on that too. You might have to fill me in there. But I'll do what I can to stop the rumors when I hear them. Bethany is a bit too excited for her own good I think." He slapped Tyson on the back. "Maybe you'd better just consider getting married if you love her. It might be easier." He chuckled to himself. "C'mon, we're gathering for pictures," he said as he walked back toward the house.

Tyson stood there for a moment longer. He certainly hadn't meant to fall in love with a Walker, but he thought maybe that was just what he'd done. Now the thought of marriage was in his head. He wasn't getting any younger, and he'd still like to have a family of his own someday. But Lydia's feelings needed to be dealt with. He couldn't hurt her like this. Family didn't hurt one another.

She'd been hurt enough. He needed to settle it.

The tension was thick, Pearl thought, but there were smiles on everyone's faces. Lydia was gracious and didn't let on that there was a problem.

Bethany had discreetly pulled Pearl to the side to congratulate her on her marriage, but Pearl had corrected her.

"That's too bad. I was very excited for you," Bethany said as she touched Pearl's arm. "Everything's okay though?"

"Yes."

"And you and Tyson?" she whispered.

Pearl didn't have it in her to lie to her. Besides, when she heard the name she couldn't help but smile. "Yeah. We've been seeing each other, though it's become a problem."

"I'm sorry."

Pearl shrugged. "Nothing to get worked up over. It'll work itself out."

A moment later, Bethany turned the conversation to Susan and Eric. That was certainly a more comfortable topic and really what the day should be about.

The photographer had taken pictures of the wedding party and the garden had filled with guests. They were moments away from walking down the aisle and watching Eric and Susan tie the knot.

Pearl had excused herself to the restroom and checked herself in the mirror one last time.

"You can't fix perfection," Tyson's voice came through the door.

She opened it and saw him leaned against the door jamb, a broad smile on his face. "You're very sweet."

He pushed open the door and stepped inside the room, closing it behind him. "I needed just a moment."

"They're going to start getting antsy."

"Only one moment." He cupped her face in his hands and gazed into her eyes. "I'm not very good at this. I've never been sentimental or able to express my feelings very well."

"So far, so good," she said, feeling her cheeks warm .

"Maybe it's the wedding atmosphere, but I wanted you to know, despite my sister's rejection of us, I really do like you."

She laughed and took his hands in hers. "I really like you too."

"I thought so. So maybe we'd better just use the right words." He leaned in and kissed her softly. "I love you."

Her heart hitched right there, and she found it hard to breathe. "You do?"

His eyes were big. "You don't feel the same way? I just did that for nothing?"

"No," she chuckled. "No. I just didn't think you felt that way. I've never had anyone feel that way about me."

"You do now."

She placed her hand over her heart. "I've been thinking about it the past few days and kept trying to talk myself out of it, but I feel the same way. But what about Lydia?"

"Lydia is a grown woman. We'll all sit down tomorrow and figure this out."

"Are you sure?"

"Today of all days, I'm most sure."

Pearl pulled him in, wrapping her arms around his neck. "I guess if that's how you feel about it, then I can tell you too. I love you."

"Good. You were starting to worry me." He nipped her lips with another soft kiss. "We'd better go."

Chapter Twenty-Six

Susan had been sucking back tears since her father had walked into the room, readied to walk her down the aisle. That had set off Bethany's tears, and Pearl had then noticed Lydia as well. To extend an olive branch, she handed her a tissue.

"Thank you," she said quickly as she dabbed at her eyes.

"You're welcome." She'd have taken it as an opportunity to work her into the first conversation all day, but it was time. They all lined up in the kitchen, ready to walk out to the garden.

As the music began, Lydia led the procession out to the altar. Pearl thought of how wonderful it was to be part of such an elegant wedding, which she'd had a hand it. It was what she lived for day in and out—helping make the perfect day for the bride.

Though, the moment she saw her cousins all lined up at the altar in their tuxedos, and not a baseball cap in sight, the tears tugged at her. This was what she did for a living. She made everything beautiful.

Of course, she'd seen Tyson already, and she couldn't help but melt when she looked at him looking so perfect in that tuxedo. Her mind flashed to the day she took the chance to push the boundaries while measuring him for the tux. It had paid off. He loved her. He'd said the words to her.

He winked as she neared the altar and she swore his eyes were moist.

Would this be where they were headed in time? Would things work out for them?

But then she heard the soft sobs of Lydia to her side.

She glanced in her direction as the guests stood to honor Susan as she walked down the aisle.

How could she put Lydia through something like this? Her commitment was to her first and foremost. The flirtation with Tyson was supposed to be just for fun. She'd never thought it would escalate to where it had.

As Susan reached the altar, she pushed it all to the back of her mind. This day was for Susan and Eric. They were lovely together, and they deserved so much happiness.

Because it was her job to do so, Pearl noticed how perfect the dress fit Susan and how perfect the earrings were that she'd chosen as an accent. Audrey had used her magic touch to transform Susan's hair into a masterpiece.

As the minister talked and Susan and Eric recited their vows, Pearl thought it was the perfect day for a wedding. She batted against the tears that threatened again as Susan and Eric kissed and were announced as man and wife.

When the intimate wedding was over, it was time to head toward town for the reception. Lydia had hurried out to be there before anyone else in the bridal party and assure her mother had everything under control. The reception was going to be much bigger than the wedding, and that was how Susan had wanted it. Lydia was determined she was going to get it.

Tyson took the opportunity to drive Pearl into town. It might be the only alone time they'd have all day.

It didn't much matter now if anyone saw them. He had to laugh at how things came to be. Everyone had learned they'd been seeing each other. Then suddenly the rumor was they were getting married, and maybe Pearl was pregnant. As an adult, he found it humorous. Either way, their relationship was in the open. Perhaps he could dance with her at the reception and hold her hand in public.

He never thought it was going to matter, but today it did. Besides, having been submerged in the Walker family and now into a wedding, he was feeling a little sentimental. There were things on his mind that had never crossed it before.

As they drove to town, they held hands. Her thumb rubbed over his knuckles, and it brought peace and warmth to him he didn't know existed.

"You'll save me a dance, won't you?" he asked, and she turned toward him.

"Of course."

"I know my sister," he began. "She won't make a scene."

"But she'll be upset."

His jaw ached from clenching it. "She's already there. We've never had a fight we couldn't talk our way out of. Tomorrow we will sit down and talk. The three of us."

"I can't help but feel as though this is my fault."

He squeezed her hand. "You can't feel like that. She's in a place where her perfect world, and mine, was shaken not too long ago. She's going on the assumption that everything will go wrong if we're together because my mom got involved once with a man who nearly lost her everything. Not getting involved with partners is the safe way, she thinks. We just need to prove her wrong."

"And how do we do that? We don't know that this will work. This is new."

"Is it?" He glanced her way and then back to the road. "I've had eyes on you for a long time."

"Then why did we wait until now?"

He shrugged. "Got me. I guess we had to let it stew."

She leaned over and rested her head on his shoulder. "I've never been one to have good timing."

Tyson chuckled. Neither had he.

~*~

Pearl had thought she'd seen the Garden Room enough times, in its different stages, to know what to expect. She'd been wrong.

Lydia and her mother had outdone themselves for Susan and Eric's wedding reception.

White lights had been strung among the vines that crept up the outer walls of the outdoor room. They shimmered as a waterfall kept a peaceful rhythm in the corner.

A string quartet played in the corner as the guests were served hors d'oeuvres and champagne by a wait staff in white coats.

"Oh, this is amazing," Pearl marveled.

She watched Tyson take in the view and the smile of pride that permeated his face was priceless.

"They are good at what they do."

"I'm going to find Bethany." Without causing a scene of any kind, she gently rested her hand on his arm and squeezed.

Tyson stood, comfortably, out of sight. Most of the guests had arrived. They were awaiting the married couple.

"Your sister has the perfect touch for this," his mother echoed Pearl's earlier statement.

Tyson looked at his mother, who was observing everything that was going on, perfectly synchronized as if it had too been rehearsed.

"You did an excellent job. Susan and Eric are going to be very pleased."

It was then she turned to him, and her eyes lost the sparkle they'd had when she spoke of the venue. "You've hurt her, you know. Your sister is miserable."

"I didn't do this to hurt her."

"You lied to her. You broke her trust."

"And tomorrow I'll fix it."

"I think it might be too late. You have no idea what your lust has done."

"Lust?" He sucked in a breath and then lowered his voice. "This isn't lust. I love Pearl."

His mother just nodded. "You think you know what love is? You're willing to risk your sister's trust in you with words like *love*?"

This wasn't happening. Not now. "I said I'd fix this tomorrow. Today it's about Eric and Susan."

"And yesterday should have been about Lydia," his mother acknowledged as she turned and walked away.

He pinched the bridge of his nose as a headache began to creep in.

So this was how it worked? He made one decision in his life, which wasn't okayed or made by his mother or his grandfather, and everything falls apart?

He'd had enough of this family time. There was a reason he worked with animals and lived in the barn.

Just as he'd decided to sneak out and leave the wedding, Eric and Susan walked through the door to grand applause.

The guests were on their feet, and the wedding party was gathering near the cake. Pearl caught his eye and waved him over.

He didn't want to be part of this anymore. He should never have been part of it, but for Eric, he stayed and joined the wedding party, which he now realized was sans his sister.

There was no time for escape, between the toast, which was made by Dane, and one by Susan's sister. Then the couple's first dance. The food was then served, and, of course, the cake.

All Tyson wanted to do was escape until a hand captured his and he turned. "I promised you a dance," Pearl insisted as she pulled him to the small dance floor where couples had gathered.

"I'm not good at this," he mused as he pulled her to him.

He was well aware of the looks coming from those that knew them. This wasn't a dance between people who were acquaintances. It was obvious there was more between them.

She pulled the daisy from her hair and tucked it into the back of his boutonniere. "A little keepsake from our first dance."

"Trust me," he whispered as he pressed his cheek to hers. "This isn't something I'll ever forget."

"Where did your sister go?"

"I don't know. Overseeing I guess."

"I didn't mean to hurt her," Pearl confessed as she looked up at him. "I'm so sorry for all of this."

Tyson shook his head. "Don't be. Don't ever be sorry for this. I love you. I told you I did."

"I know, but…"

"No buts. There has to be a time when I get to make my own decisions. And I've decided to make one."

"But at what cost?"

He pulled her to the corner where it was dark and private. "She's going to let this go. I won't let this become a problem. I gave her my word, and I broke it. But I'll fix it."

Pearl smiled as she eased against him again. "And what decision did you come to that is going to be all yours?"

"I think we should get married."

Pearl staggered back and looked up at him. "You what?"

"Wrong decision?"

"Unexpected one."

"You said you didn't want all of this," he motioned to the room and the people around them. "You wanted something private."

"A marriage isn't the wedding."

"I understand that." He let out a ragged breath. "Listen, I love you. That much I know." He gathered her hands. "I'm not versed in people skills, such as you are. I don't have a family like yours that rallies around one another. I only have Lydia, but I can manage her."

"Manage?"

"Pearl, I'm trying to be somewhat romantic here. I want to marry you. I want to take off and do it just as you said you wanted to. Just the two of us."

Her eyes went moist as she lifted her hands to his face. "I didn't expect this," she sighed. "I love you. But I can't let this tear apart your family."

The tears streamed down her face now, and he realized he was frozen. He couldn't even wipe them away.

"What are you saying?"

"I can't. I can't marry you." She'd taken a breath as if she had more to say, but she didn't. She only turned away and ran out of the Garden Room and disappeared.

Chapter Twenty-Seven

No one had called. No one had stopped by. Somehow she'd missed everyone's radar when she'd run out of Susan and Eric's wedding.

She'd let her cell phone die and stayed off her computer and social media all Sunday.

The only person she'd expected to hear from was Tyson, but even he hadn't come around.

For the first time in her life, she hated going into work on Monday morning. Had she not scheduled an appointment with a bride at ten, she would have sulked and stayed in bed. As it was, she dragged herself to work in her best suit hoping it would shroud her in professionalism.

The bride had called and rescheduled her appointment, which irritated Pearl though she understood. Later that day she knew someone would be coming in with all the tuxedos from Eric's wedding party. Of course, the thought had crossed her mind, would it be Tyson?

After the UPS driver, the Fed Ex driver, and the postal carrier had dropped off packages at her store, the door opened again. When she looked up, she couldn't help but smile when she saw Sunshine walk through. Her father had been right to name her that. She undoubtedly brought the sunshine into people's lives.

"It's nice to see you," Pearl said as she moved from behind her counter toward her.

"I stopped by to bring you another thank you note." She handed her another envelope with her name written in calligraphy. "The flowers you sent were very thoughtful. My uncle might stop by to thank you as well. He was very moved."

"It was my pleasure. I was so sorry to hear about your father's passing."

"Thank you. It was hard to watch him the last week. It just all went so quickly," she spoke softly. "But we were all there with him."

"That's important."

"Your friend Lydia was at the services yesterday. My uncle introduced us. Her brother was with her."

Hearing that stabbed into Pearl's chest. She'd been so preoccupied with feeling sorry for herself, she hadn't even realized that Sunshine's father's services were yesterday. She'd planned to go.

But hearing that he was with Lydia solidified her choice. She'd been right to reject his proposal. Lydia was more important.

"I'm glad they were there," she managed without the emotion shaking her voice.

"My mom didn't let me in on it, but she said it was a big deal to have Lydia there."

Pearl just nodded. Having Lydia purposely go where Phillip Smythe would be was a big thing.

Sunshine looked around the store. "It's quiet in here today."

"My appointment canceled. I've been taking inventory so I can plan for the move next month."

"That's very exciting. You know, I'm in between jobs right now. If you ever need help, let me know. I owe you for what you've done for me."

Pearl thought, for only a brief moment. "Do you mean that?"

"Of course."

"I've been thinking about the need to hire someone to help out. First of all, I'm all alone. So I don't take any time off. Which is okay. That's by design too. But with the new store, I'll need to divide my time to oversee its construction. Having someone around would be a blessing."

Sunshine's face lit. "Whatever you need. I'm your girl. I love all this stuff. I'm a quick study too."

For the first time since she'd walked away from Tyson, Pearl smiled. "C'mon, let's have a crash course in fittings."

The afternoon had taken a turn, that was for sure. Pearl and Sunshine had *played* dress up.

She let Sunshine pick out a dress to try on and then walked her through clipping it so that the bride could see what it would look like fitted correctly.

"Now you," Sunshine said. "Let me try."

Pearl bit down on her bottom lip. "I have one."

She retrieved the dress she'd always kept *in case*. It had been a long time since she'd tried it on and now it only made her sad to retrieve it. But for Sunshine, she did.

Feeling the satin under her fingers again only made her long for Tyson. She held back the tears that threatened. It wasn't meant to be, she thought.

Sliding the dress over her body, she thought back to the day the dress had come into the store. She'd unpackaged it and promptly put it on a mannequin in the front window. It was her mother that stopped a few days later and told her it wasn't pretty enough.

Pearl had looked at it before she'd undressed the mannequin. Her mother was right. It wasn't pretty. It was elegant.

There wasn't much fuss to it. It was a straight skirt and off the shoulders. The lace that defined the neckline was minimal, but oh, so elegant.

It was exactly what Pearl had always wanted. Nothing too fancy. Something that she could wear in her untraditional wedding, should she ever have one.

"C'mon. I want to see," Sunshine's voice chimed from the other room.

Pearl stepped out, and Sunshine's hands went straight to her mouth. "Oh-my-word. You are stunning."

"I don't know about that. This is eight years old now."

"It's the most beautiful dress I've ever seen."

Pearl stood on the platform in front of the three-way mirror and looked at herself. It was the most beautiful dress she'd ever seen too.

"What kind of veil?" Sunshine asked walking toward the rack.

"No veil," Pearl said, still studying herself in the mirror. "Only a ring of daisies."

Sunshine rested her hands on her chest. "Yes. That's it."

When the door opened, they both turned to see Bethany walking through with Susan's sister. Each had an armload of tuxedos.

Bethany stopped. "Oh, look at you."

Pearl was quick to move from her pedestal. "We're just trying on dresses."

"I'm learning how to fit them," Sunshine said.

But Bethany's eyes didn't wander. "Pearl, it's exquisite. You look fabulous."

"Thank you. It's something I've saved." She moved toward them. "Let me take those from you."

Sunshine followed suit and took the stack Susan's sister carried.

"They're all there," Bethany said. "Dane thinks his bow tie is in a pocket. If you don't have it let him know."

She laughed. Usually, that was the most lost item.

"Did Susan and Eric leave for their honeymoon?"

"Yes," Susan's sister said. "Eric was quite nervous to leave everything behind. But I think he'll get over it when his toes are in the sand."

Pearl felt the pang of sadness creep through her.

Bethany and Susan's sister visited for a bit longer, and then they were off to finish tying up the small details of after wedding items.

Pearl changed out of the wedding dress, hung it back in its bag, and back on the save rack in the back room. Then she went about teaching Sunshine how to catalog the tuxedos that were returned so that they could ship them back.

"At the new store I'll have room to carry a small selection of rental tuxedos," she told Sunshine.

"That's very exciting. I'm really happy for you. It must be wonderful to work in a field that you love."

"It is."

She took down the next tuxedo from the rack and immediately she knew it had been Tyson's. She could smell his cologne lingering on it.

It took every ounce of willpower not to bring it to her nose and linger in the smell.

As was the process, she checked the buttons and the fabric for any damage. Then she slid her hands, carefully, into each pocket.

Inside the tuxedo pocket was the daisy she'd tucked into his lapel with his boutonniere last night. Wrapped around the stem was a small, jagged piece of paper. *I'll never forget* was written across it.

Tears immediately began to choke her, and she fought them off, but to no avail.

"Pearl, what's wrong?" Sunshine quickly moved to her with a tissue she'd pulled from the box. "Is everything okay? Are you alright?"

Pearl nodded as she dabbed her eyes. "I'm sorry."

Sunshine noticed the flower and the note. "Did that mean something?" she asked.

"For a very short time." For the first time all day, her cell phone rang, and she was glad to have the distraction. "Hey, Donald," she answered and listened to the very excited man tell her he needed her at the new location A.S.A.P. "Can it wait until I'm done here?" She nodded as he protested. "I'll be there in half an hour," she promised as she disconnected the phone.

"What can I help with?" Sunshine was already standing there waiting for direction.

"Do you think you can just watch the store for an hour? I have to run to the new location. I won't be long, and we don't have anything going on today."

"I'll be fine," Sunshine said as she reached for Pearl's hands. "Take your time. I've decided that this is where I need to be. With you. You are in need of some time and not just an hour to run and take care of things. I want you to know you can count on me."

"I appreciate that. I'll work on letting go a little," she chuckled. "I'll be back in an hour."

Chapter Twenty-Eight

Pearl could see Donald inside the shop before she arrived. He had swatches laid out on the floor and his design book open on his lap.

She walked through the door, and he jumped to his feet. "Oh goodie, you're here. Lydia let me in. We were working on the reception hall. O.M.G. you're going to die when you see it."

"I'm sure it's going to be amazing."

"Uh-huh!" He pulled her into his arms and kissed her on the cheek. "I heard about your breakup."

That meant Tyson had talked to Lydia as he'd said he was going to. If he were going to handle it, she would have thought they'd have come to discuss it with her. Instead, it had been given the finality of a breakup. That was fine. That was essentially what had happened.

"It kills me. He's so sexy," Donald added with a pout.

Pearl stepped back. "It's fine. Really. So what do you want to show me?"

Donald went to work and began showing Pearl the swatches he'd put together for flooring, paint, and furniture. She was sure, in the end, that trust fund she'd joked about was going to be toast.

His ideas were genius. There was a reason her mother always used him in everything she did.

Donald's phone rang near the end of his presentation. "Another job. I'm just the golden child of design these days," he marveled at himself. "I'll just pick this up and head out. We start on Monday."

"Really? That soon?"

"Darling, if we don't get a move on, we will not be ready for your big opening. Lydia and I have been planning it. Gia

Gallow is even making a special trip back to Italy to get some new goodies for her store. Oh, this is going to be lovely!"

She watched him hurry about, and then he kissed her before he ran out the door. Suddenly, she was alone in her new space.

Pearl sat down in the middle of the empty room and let the silence surround her. This was what she'd always wanted. It was going to be the most amazing store ever.

But there was something missing.

She didn't want to think about it. Her heart was broken, and she'd done it to herself. But she couldn't see Tyson and Lydia losing what they had. Pearl already felt as though her parents weren't a big part of her life. What would happen if her sisters and brothers disappeared too?

Tyson and Lydia needed each other, and if that meant she stepped out of the way, then she would do it.

Pearl turned her head to the door when she heard footsteps.

"I saw Donald leave. I just came to lock up," Lydia said softly as if she were afraid to speak to Pearl.

"I'm done." Pearl stood.

Lydia moved inside and shut the door behind her. "I think we should talk."

"We're fine. Really. You and I are partners, and we need to just move on as such."

Lydia shook her head. "I heard what you did."

"I didn't do anything except go behind your back." Guilt churned in her stomach. "We knew how you felt about everything, and we went with our lust. I guess the old Pearl is still in there. I didn't think about anything but myself."

Lydia walked in closer. "I don't think so." She tucked her hands into the back pockets of her paint-stained overalls. "Yes, you both lied to me. You hid something from me that I felt adamant about."

"See? The old Pearl. Not someone you probably want to be friends with, let alone partners."

"On the contrary." She kicked her foot against the bare floor. "I tried love once, and it didn't work out. I supplemented that loss with business."

Pearl understood that concept very well.

Lydia looked around the bare room as if to keep her eyes focused away from Pearl. "So my mom made mistakes. I made that personal. I used it against you and Tyson. I needed his investment."

"We're all partners. Lydia, it's okay."

"He loves you."

"It was an affair. A quick affair that didn't net any bonuses," she said as convincingly as she could.

"He told me he proposed."

"Out of spite, I'm sure."

Lydia shook her head again and looked at Pearl. "He'd never do that. I want to offer you my share of the business for free rent. We can work out numbers later. But then you and Tyson will own the building, and I won't be in the way."

Pearl moved to her and pulled her into her arms. "You were my partner first. Tyson and I will recover. I will never, ever come between a brother and sister. I will not be the reason a family gets torn apart."

"He's miserable," Lydia whispered in Pearl's ear.

"He won't be miserable forever."

"I'm not so sure about that," Tyson's voice rumbled from the doorway.

Pearl and Lydia stepped apart.

"Lydia and I were just talking business," Pearl's voice shook.

"Cutting me out?" He shoved his hands into his front pockets and leaned against the door jamb as he'd done so many times before.

"If you want out, I'll find the financing," she offered.

"I didn't say I did." He walked toward them. He stood behind Lydia and placed his hands on her shoulders. They both focused on Pearl. "Family is very important to both of us."

"I understand that. That's why I didn't accept your proposal. I won't be the reason you two are torn apart. There have been too many lies told, and I don't want to be a part of that anymore. Like you said, we weren't any better than our own parents."

He stepped around Lydia and closer to her. "Lydia," he said without looking at her. "Did you ask her about the buyout for free rent?"

"Of course."

Pearl narrowed her eyes on him. "You knew about that?"

"I thought it was a fair trade. Crunch the numbers. It works in her favor."

Pearl swallowed hard. "I don't understand what's going on."

He reached for her hands, and she fought the urge to tug them back, but his skin on her skin felt so nice.

"Lydia and I, we're as tight as a family can get. The Walkers, well, they're a tight-knit group. Seems as though we're supposed to all be family." He raised his hand to her cheek. "We want you to be part of our family."

She looked at Lydia, who was now wiping away tears and then back to Tyson. "What do you mean?"

"I mean my proposal still stands, with Lydia's blessing. Will you marry me?"

Pearl batted against the tears that stung her eyes and then looked at Lydia who encouraged her by nodding her head. "I was wrong," she whispered. "Marry the man. Be my sister. I hadn't looked at it like that. It's even better than a business partner."

Now the tears burst through, and she couldn't control them.

"I love you."

He smiled and brushed away the tears with his thumb. "I know. That's why I'm standing here asking you to marry me again. But I'm kind of afraid you're going to turn me down again."

She shook her head. "No. No, I won't turn you down," she stuttered as she tried to control the tears.

"Is that a very bad way to say yes?" he joked.

"Yes."

He pulled her in and pressed his warm lips to her trembling ones. He pulled back and reached into his pocket. "This is for you," he said holding up an older bridal set between his fingers. "My mother and father were very happily married until he died. She says that marriage is an amazing thing to enter into with the person you love."

"You told your mother?"

He shrugged. "No more secrets." He took her hand and slid the ring on her finger. "She wants you to have it, but would understand if you decided against it."

Pearl looked at Lydia. "What about you? This should be yours."

"I'm not getting married. Remember? I traded love for business."

She was finding it hard to catch her breath. "This has all been so sudden."

Lydia burst out with a laugh. "Are you kidding me? He's been in love with you for a very long time."

He nudged Lydia. "She doesn't need to know everything."

Pearl laughed now. "No secrets."

He kissed her softly. "Never, ever again."

Epilogue

Bethany's dress had been sent out for final alterations. The men in her bridal party had been fitted for their tuxes.

Sunshine walked out of the storage room with a tape measure draped around her neck. "I just checked in all the tuxes for next weekend."

Pearl nodded as she checked her calendar on the computer. "A new bride is looking to come in next weekend, but I won't be here."

Sunshine moved in next to her and nudged her out of the way. "I have fitted thirty brides in the past two months. I can fit another. You are going to go and get married and get out of my hair," she demanded with a smile while entering the information into the calendar.

Pearl had indeed made the right decision in hiring Sunshine. She wondered what she'd ever done without her.

"I think I should tell Tyson that we have to move this. I mean, it's silly to get married the week before my sister does."

"Don't you dare cancel on me," he said from the dressing area.

She turned to see him standing there in a tuxedo, his baseball cap and boots still on. "I might if you don't change your shoes or your hat."

He cocked an eyebrow. "Don't you love me the way I am?"

Pearl moved to him. "I love you in every way." She kissed him softly. "Does it fit?"

"You felt me up to measure me for it. I don't know why you couldn't just use the measurements from before."

"I love what I do," she said with a wink.

"You two better get that tux and dress loaded into the car. Your flight leaves in four hours," Sunshine instructed.

"She's right, we'd better go. There's a Hawaiian sunset waiting for us, and only us," Pearl beamed. "Let me just get my dress."

I hope you enjoyed the third installment of

The Walker Family Series.

Here is a preview of book four
WANDERLUST

Chapter One ~ Wanderlust

Horses had a way of knowing when a person needed peace. Fairy Godmother was that kind of horse, Dane thought as she stood in the middle of the pasture and let Dane take in the peace of the moment.

He was back in Georgia for another family wedding. That was three weddings in two months, although no one had attended Pearl and Tyson's wedding.

As he'd packed his bag for this journey, he'd quietly thanked them for not making anyone else reschedule their lives. But now that he was home, he was glad he'd come.

Ohio wasn't his kind of place. His job wasn't his kind of job. Somewhere his life hadn't become his either.

He now found that he envied his brother Eric for getting married and staying at home on the land they called theirs. Their father had promised them all they could build a house there if they wanted. All that time Dane had refused. There had to be more for him, he thought. But now he just wasn't so sure.

The sound of a rider was coming up from behind him. No doubt it would be Lydia, who housed her horses at the Walker's barn, taking her morning ride, he thought as he turned Fairy Godmother toward the sound.

With the sun to the rider's back, he could only see her outline, but it wasn't Lydia. A high ponytail swung behind the rider who was obviously new to the saddle. He wondered who had let her wander off.

As the rider drew near, she waved. "Hello."

"Hi," he called back.

"Beautiful morning."

Her accent was familiar, but he had to think to where he knew her from. But the moment she came into full view, he remembered.

"Gia, right?" he asked, hoping that was, in fact, her name.

"Gia Gallow. You are correct. And you are Dane." There was no question in her voice. She'd remembered him.

"Dane Walker," he mimicked James Bond when he said it.

"I met you at Pearl's dress shop a few months ago."

"I remember."

"I assume you're here for Bethany's wedding."

"I am. I guess if all my cousins and brothers keep getting married, I'll be visiting a lot."

Her horse moved quickly, and Dane was ready to adjust on Fairy Godmother to help her out, but she got the horse under control and just smiled at him.

"He is a fidgety one, Mr. Melancholy."

"Mr. Melancholy?" he chuckled. "Eric gave me a hard time about my horse's name."

"Brothers are like that. I have knowledge that he named this one himself. I would not let him judge you on the name of your horse."

He eased back in the saddle. "I'll keep it in mind for when I need to pick a fight."

"Well, I only have another half hour before they will come looking for me. Besides, I need to get back into town and go to work."

"You have the Italian gift store, right?"

She smiled that beautiful smile that he knew was fueled by pride. "You remember."

"I know that it was mentioned that you moved into the same building with Susan, Pearl, and Lydia."

"I did." She nudged Mr. Melancholy closer to Fairy Godmother. "Will you be in town this week?"

He shrugged. "Maybe."

"Drop by. I would love to give you a tour of my shop." With a wink, she turned Mr. Melancholy around and headed back to the barn.

Dane remained in the pasture watching her disappear. The thought to ride after her only entered his mind after he couldn't see her any longer. But he knew it was a bad idea. First of all, riding up on her would spook Mr. Melancholy, and he'd toss her. Second, there was no need to get worked up over the beautiful Italian woman. He was heading back to the hell known as Ohio on Monday. He might as well forget about Gia Gallow.

Meet the Author

Bestselling Author Bernadette Marie is known for building families readers want to be part of. Her series *The Keller Family* has graced bestseller charts since its release in 2011, along with her other series and single title books. The married mother of five sons promises *Happily Ever After always*...and says she can write it, because she lives it.

When not writing, Bernadette Marie is shuffling her sons to their many events—mostly hockey—and enjoying the beautiful views of the Colorado Rocky Mountains from her front step. She is also an accomplished martial artist with a second degree black belt in Tang Soo Do.

A chronic entrepreneur, Bernadette Marie opened her own publishing house in 2011, *5 Prince Publishing*, so that she could publish the books she liked to write and help make the dreams of other aspiring authors come true too. Bernadette Marie is also the CEO of *Illumination Author Events and Services*.